JAMI ROGERS

To all my readers who fell in love with Always Been Write and Promise Me ... here are their siblings!

Loving you

JAMI ROGERS

PROLOGUE

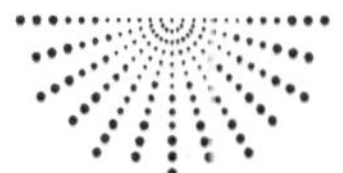

QUINN – LAST SUMMER

I hate to admit this, but faking a smile isn't as easy as it used to be.

"Yes! Yes! Yes!"

Andy, my friend—or travel acquaintance, or whatever you want to call her—wraps her arms around her boyfriend's neck and kisses him over and over.

He stands from where he'd been down on his knee in the sand and kisses her back.

The friends around us are clapping and cheering. I hear a bottle of champagne pop somewhere.

It's clear that some of the people here knew this was about to happen and some didn't.

I'm in the group who didn't know, but that's fine. I have travel friends, and I have real friends, and right now, I'm surrounded by travel friends.

That's not to say that my travel friends aren't real—we just have a different kind of relationship. We take trains, boats, and planes all over the world to see new places. I post all about my trips and get paid for it.

Right now, we're on the beach in Lefkada Island, Greece. It's absolute heaven and one of my favorite places to visit. I've been here three times now, and I came back this time not for work but because Andy, the new bride, invited me. I was about to head back to the States for the summer, but something told me one more week would be worth it. I could sit on pretty beaches and let the sun kiss my skin and relax me. The pictures I'd take would be my own, and I didn't have to do anything I didn't want to do. It would be the perfect short break to remind myself why I love what I do. Until this moment, it has been all of those things.

Don't get me wrong, I love that this is happening for her, but the exact moment she screams out the third yes is when I realize I'm officially surrounded by couples.

I instantly feel out of place as each couple greets the happy pair two by two.

After I see the last one approaching, I stand, dusting the white sand from my legs as I make my way over to them.

"Can you believe it?" Andy gushes, holding out her hand to admire the square rock on her finger.

"It's gorgeous," Ashley, who I've only met a handful of times, says, and the other girls who came with Andy agree with her.

"It's perfect for you," I say, grabbing her hand.

Out of all the girls gushing over the diamond, I know Andy the best. We've traveled a lot together. After that it's Ashley. The others I just met this week.

The guys huddle up, doing their typical man thing where they slap each other on the shoulder and tease each other over their newfound happiness, secretly super excited for one another.

I have an older brother, and I've watched as he and his friends all did the same exact thing as they fell in love. I get it. One day you're living your life to the fullest and depending on no one, and then bam! Someone walks in and all of the sudden, you can't think straight. If you think about making a sandwich, you're simultaneously wondering whether they would like one, too, and maybe you should call them. Then before you know it, your every waking thought is about someone else, and it's hard to admit how vulnerable that makes you.

At this point, even though those things haven't happened to me, I feel like I've lived it a dozen times.

"We should go out for girls' night to celebrate," Ashley says, and Andy instantly nods.

"Let's tell the boys that they are on their own tonight."

Each girl runs off, sharing quick words with their other halves, and then we all head back to the resort to clean up for the night. Swimsuits clearly aren't the vibe we want to keep through the evening.

As the girls walk ahead of me, I pull out my phone to snap a picture of the clear blue water.

I'd rather sit here and soak up the fact that a view like this isn't something we should ever take for granted, but then again, a girl only gets engaged for the first time once.

I quickly type out a caption for my social media page and tag the location. I have to jog a little to catch up with the girls.

Unlike the rest of them, I'm not out here traveling off Mommy and Daddy's money. I'm here because I traveled so much with my parents when I was younger that when my social media page took off, brands and businesses reached out to me to talk about their products or visit their locations. It's fun, yes, but almost everywhere I go, I'm working.

Which is exactly why I love going to the States during the summer. I spend two, sometimes three, months with my grandmother in her small town of Lovers, Wyoming. The entire time I'm there, I get to enjoy myself, and that's all that is required of me.

"Now we just have to find a man for Quinny and the group trips will take on an entirely new vibe," Ashley says.

Oh, here we go. This conversation, *again*.

And don't even get me started on "Quinny."

Ick.

I hate to sound ungrateful, because I truly feel like they all say this out of love, but it's exhausting to hear them talk about this at every engagement.

"Oh, let's not talk about anything but Andy and Sully. I'm so happy for you," I say. It's Andy's night, not mine.

"But you're the last one of us not engaged," Ashley goes on. "What about Sully's brother, Danny? He's always fighting for your attention."

I ignore everything about her statement. Danny and me … ugh, I hate being wine drunk. That is a night I never want to relive again, and Danny needs to accept that I told him friends is all we could ever be.

"Don't you want this?" Chancy asks.

"Not to mention, it gets lonely traveling alone," Ashley adds, and the other girls nod, choosing this moment to add to the conversation.

"Going home to someone really is the best feeling."

"And the late-night phone calls."

"Oh, and the good morning text messages."

"Yes, I agree."

"Come one, Quinny, don't you think that having a guy in your life to share these memories with would be fun?" Andy asks, stopping the entire group before we part ways to our rooms.

Instantly, all eyes are on me.

I'm like a walking contradiction, because although I have a social media following with millions of followers, I hate when the attention is on me.

"Yeah, to sleep next to and wake up next to and talk to all day and night and—"

"I do have that," I blurt out and then cross my arms to cover the goose bumps that break out on my skin. On the beach, my bikini and sarong was fitting, but in this hallway it's like the dead of winter in Wyoming. Or maybe it's just the thick weight of the lie I just told.

"You do?" Andy asks with the biggest smile on her face.

I nod as bile creeps its way into my throat.

God, I hate lying, but let's be real, once this trip is over, I won't see these girls for at least six months, and I can easily have endured a breakup in that time.

"That's amazing!" She wraps her arms around me. "Why haven't we met him?"

That's a good question. I force another smile and think of why they haven't met this new imaginary boyfriend of mine that gives me all the gooey feelings.

"He doesn't like to travel," I say because it feels like a perfect explanation.

They all pause in shock.

"He doesn't?"

I shake my head.

"Why not?"

Sheesh. I should have known the questions wouldn't stop.

"Because it's nice to date someone who is the complete opposite of me," I say, proud of my quick thinking.

Andy smiles with a nod like she gets it.

"What's his name?" Ashley asks, and truthfully, I'm starting to not enjoy hanging out with her. She's pretty damn nosey.

I take a deep breath, my mind running through all the details I've just told them, and instantly one man comes to mine.

He really does hate to travel, and he really is the complete opposite of me. He also lives in the same small town as my grandmother. The chances of these girls ever meeting him is extra slim.

No one will ever know I'm lying, and after tonight, I can forget all about this moment.

So I hold my head high, smile for real, and I give them a name.

"Miles. His name is Miles."

CHAPTER ONE

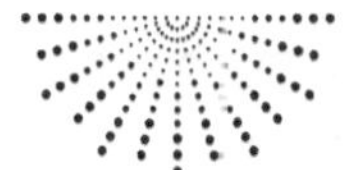

MILES - PRESENT DAY

What tip would you give to someone who lives, or is planning to live, in a small touristy town?

This is an easy one.

Don't fool around with the vacationers.

Don't even hit on them, flirt, buy drinks, or ask for their phone number.

Do. Not. Engage.

That would be my answer.

Unfortunately, I never asked this question, so I never got an answer. Last summer … well, let's just say my plans for *this* summer do not include getting involved with someone who doesn't plan to settle down in my small town of Lovers, Wyoming. Especially not someone who thinks that returning for the summer means we pick up right where we left off.

I'm a small-town lifer, and I can say that with confidence.

"Is the beer stale?"

I glance up to find my older brother, Hudson, glaring at me.

He owns the bar where I'm currently having lunch. In the last year, it's become a bar slash romance bookstore with

Sadie, his very new fiancée. I still can't believe those two are together, let alone engaged. Last summer was one for the books, and Hudson very well might be the only Asher brother who didn't do something to fuck it up. Hence, even though he's glaring at me, I know he's happier than he's ever been in his entire life.

And yes, I am having a beer in the middle of the day on my lunch break because I own my business, a thriving one, and I can do whatever the fuck I want.

"No." I proceed to take a sip, trying not to let the stress of my day or the grumpiness of my current life situation shine through my tone.

My brother crosses his arms and nods toward me. "Then why is your forehead all wrinkled and the rest of your face pissed off?"

I avoid his gaze. Along with my brother's newfound happiness comes his rekindled love for his brothers and little sister. That's me, my twin brother Luca, and Ruby. Ruby doesn't live here anymore, though, so lucky for me and Luca, Hudson has made it a point this last year to be in our business. And clearly, no matter how hard I try, I can't hide anything from him anymore.

Considering he pushed us away for years, I have a love-hate relationship with this topic. I missed the hell out of him, but I love my space, and he's been crowding it with his stupid, smiling face every single day for the last year.

"That's just the way I look," I tell him and pop a fry into my mouth.

It's not a lie. Hudson has always been known to be the serious one of the family. Luca is the goofy one. Ruby is the sweetheart. And me…well, I'm the moody one. You could ask anyone in our town to confirm this, and they would agree.

It's not a crime that I like what I like and am honest about it.

Being blunt or truthful shouldn't make me a dick, but somehow it does.

He shakes his head slowly. "Sure. Or it's because tourist season is here, and it's about to get busy, which means certain people will be back."

I refuse to look at him.

One year. One fucking year was all it took for him to remember how to read me like a book.

"That's not it," I say, and he barks out a laugh.

He leans to the bar top, resting on his forearms. "Sure as shit it is."

I groan.

"Maybe you'll get lucky, and she won't return this summer."

Now it's my turn to laugh.

"Considering she texts me weekly to check in and let me know she's still planning to come, I don't agree with you."

I pull my phone from my pocket to show him the unread message I received this morning.

He glances at my phone and then stands tall, grabs a ticket off the printer, and starts to make a drink in front of me. "Tell her you don't want to see her."

"I have. Either my text messages aren't going through, or she can't read. And before you suggest it, I'm not calling her."

Even though people think I'm a dick, I don't try to be. And this situation is complicated. I'd be stuck on the phone with her for far longer than I want. Hudson knows it.

"You're not calling who?" Luca pulls up the chair next to me. He reaches for my plate and slides it toward himself. I already ate the burger, so all that's left are fries, and now they are clearly his fries.

It's okay, though. I've suddenly lost my appetite.

"Cherry," Hudson answers before I can reroute this conversation.

I close my eyes and take a deep breath.

Yep, that's her name. The tourist from last summer. Cherry Lucial Pepperton, to be exact.

Shit. Her full name alone should have told me to run and never look back.

I'm chalking it up to a weak moment.

I was watching my brother fall in love, and perhaps a tiny piece of me wanted that, too.

Unlucky for me, though, I went searching in the wrong place.

"Oooh, not Cherry," Luca says and makes an absurd noise next to me. I punch his shoulder.

"Fuck. Ouch," he says with a laugh. "You two made fun of me for three years over one of my hookups. This is just payback."

"This is different," I snap.

"How so?"

"Cherry is coming back this summer, and Miles here,"—Hudson grins—"is super looking forward to it."

"No, I'm not looking forward to it. I'm dreading it. She can't take a hint, and I have no idea what I'm going to do."

Add to that the fact that the apartment I built for my dad behind my mechanic shop is still empty because he isn't ready to move out of his house yet, I'm three months behind on the books for my shop, and I need a shop hand to help me get caught up. The list of shit I need to accomplish is growing fast. The last thing I need is Cherry showing up at the shop every single day and asking me to hang out.

Not to mention, if a tourist, namely Cherry, gets wind of the apartment being for rent before I can find a tenant, I'm screwed. I'd take it off the market, but my plan is to pressure my dad to move in now by leasing it to someone else. I know it sounds terrible, but his house is too big for him, and whether we want to admit it or not, he's getting older. He doesn't need a tri-level home with his bedroom upstairs and the laundry in the basement.

I'm just being practical.

As for the rest, well, I need help, but it's no secret asking for help is not something that comes easily to the Asher family, which is exactly why I'm behind.

I blow out a breath and get up.

"I should get back to work. I need to keep my mind busy."

I take a twenty from my wallet and place it on the bar top before telling my brothers goodbye and walking out the door onto Main Street.

Lovers isn't a big town. The only reason it's so successful and busy is because of Lovers Lake and Lovers Lodge next to it. The lodge is known as one of the most elite locations for weddings. More celebrities have been married there than the non-famous type. Once, out of curiosity, I looked into the pricing, and truth be told, despite its glamour and reputation, it's not as expensive as I would have imagined.

I glance to my right, where the lodge sits, just past the end of Main Street. It's close enough to be a part of our town but far enough away to give the locals and tourists space to breathe. That said, those damn tourists love to flock into town all damn day long and year-round.

I'm not ungrateful for them. I own the only mechanic shop in Lovers, so anyone who travels here and needs something comes to me. Plus, I'm pretty damn good at restoring classic cars, and when some of the wealthier visitors notice, they provide me business all year round. One especially has brought me more business than I ever imagined. I'm pretty sure he could take it away just as fast as it came.

I don't have social media or anything to show my work, so I think many of my customers also love the discretion I can offer them.

Speaking of work, I now have two cars in my shop that need my attention. If all goes right, one will be finished today.

I head in the opposite direction of the lodge toward my shop, but I only make it one door over from the bar. B's Bakery has the best treats, and I like the reward at the end of the day, so I dip inside.

My brothers tease me that the sweets and baked goods will catch up with me one day, but I don't care. My mom used to bring me a sweet treat anytime I finished a goal. Whether it was for school or fixing up cars, she always noticed and would appear with something to celebrate my hard work. Even though she passed away when I was fifteen, and I'm almost thirty-one now, I'm pretty sure she'd love that I kept our tradition and continue to do this for myself.

"Surprise, surprise," Brooke says the moment I step into her sugary wonderland. Brooke, also known as Sadie's best friend, bought the bakery from Sadie at the end of last summer. It's a long story, a pretty great one if you ask me, but Brooke is the perfect person to own this shop.

"I'm a creature of habit," I say just as I notice Sadie sitting in the corner. "Afternoon there, sister-in-law."

She beams a smile. "Technically, not yet."

"Technically, that doesn't matter to me."

She rolls her eyes and goes back to her laptop.

"I'm not sure I'll ever get past the fact that I never noticed how flirty your entire family can be."

"Um, did you just accuse me of flirting with my brother's fiancée?" I cross my arms.

Sadie smirks. "Can you call me that one more time?"

"What? You are the fiancée to my brother, Hudson Asher, right?"

"Oh my god, can you two stop?" Brooke groans. "She

doesn't need to be reminded. He's already been here three times to practically make out with her while she works."

"Why aren't you doing this work at the bookstore?"

"Because of what Brooke said. At least here it's only little pop-ins. If I were next door, then it would be back-room visits, and those are—"

"I got it. No need to finish that sentence." I chuckle and then point to the caramel brownie bites in the display. "I'll take three of those."

"Three," Brooke shrieks. "You always get two of something. Always. Just two."

"What's going on? Are you okay?" Sadie chimes in, rising from her seat to stand beside me.

"Nothing is wrong." I grab my wallet to pay for the food.

Brooke slowly puts my treats in a bag and hands it to me.

"Is it because your dad doesn't want to move into the apartment you built him?" Sadie asks.

I glance at her, but I don't say anything.

"Or because it's tourist season?"

I'm not surprised that Hudson shares every little detail with her, but it still makes me curious to know where he would draw the line.

"Is there anything my brother doesn't share with you?" I ask.

She nods. "Nope. Believe it or not, we do find time to talk … occasionally."

Brooke snorts, and I groan. "I'm fine."

Sadie's gaze narrows as if she doesn't believe me. "Just take it off the market if you don't want Cherry to see it."

I sigh. It really is the only way to guarantee she doesn't see it. And truth be told, there isn't a single local looking to move, so either I rent it to a tourist, or it sits empty until my dad is ready.

I nod. "Yeah, I'll call Linc this afternoon."

Linc is both Sadie's brother and Hudson's best friend.

As I said, Lovers is a small town, and Linc and Mr. Collins, Sadie's dad, own the only real-estate company here.

I tell the girls goodbye on my way out the door.

Not only is my shop at the opposite end of Main Street from the lodge, it's one block over. It gives me just enough privacy but still lets me walk everywhere I need to in town.

I reach the shop but walk past it, then past the apartment built on the back and across the small yard to my new house.

I've done a lot of building in the last couple of years. It helps that Luca owns his own contractor company here in town.

I put my brownies in the fridge and then return to the shop to get to work. I really should step into the office to do some invoicing, but my hands itch to work on the baby-blue 1968 Chevy Chevelle SS in front of me.

As I pause to admire the car, my phone starts to go off repeatedly.

I loathe group texts.

I grab my phone to see a fuzzy picture from Luca. He's clearly hiding to take this picture, and despite the grainy look, it's clear as day to me.

Cherry is back in Lovers.

Officially.

Fuck.

I hate being stressed, and adding her presence to a life I already feel is out of control gets under my skin.

I just need to stick to the shop and keep my head down. If I stay busy, I won't have time for anything or anyone.

Sure, I might miss out on some of the town's festivals and other fun events, and it'll suck not to see my brothers if I lock myself in my house or the shop and get caught up on life, but it'll be worth it.

Yeah.

I'll just keep to myself.

It's not like my summer can get much worse than this, right?

CHAPTER TWO

QUINN

I am completely out of my element right now.

I love babies, but as someone who hasn't spent much time around them, holy cannoli, they cry a lot. At night, too. All the time, really, especially when they are six months old. Babies are a lot of work.

And the best part about my situation is that my brother and his wife have two of them.

Twins.

Ha.

"I'm so happy to have you home for the summer, dear," Grandma Betty whispers as she pats my knee.

We are sitting in my brother's living room with no music, no TV, and all phones on silent. Natalie, my sister-in-law, just went up to get some sleep, and my brother Tobias is quietly trying to clean so that Natalie doesn't think about the dishes or any other mess when she wakes up.

If you ask me, he needs sleep, too, but that man would stay awake for days if it meant he could do something, anything, for his wife.

They are increasingly disgustingly in love each day, and I envy every single moment of it.

"Me too," I whisper back and then lean into my grandmother.

I flew in from London a few days ago, and even though I love returning to Lovers over the summer, I'm not sure I can stay here much longer. In this house, to be more specific.

Yes, I could suck it up for the babies, but for three days, I've asked to help make things easier for them, but Natalie and Tobias keep telling me no thanks. At this point, I feel like I'm just in the way. And for someone who was already starting to feel a little like she doesn't really have a purpose in life anymore, that feeling of not being needed sucks.

I could stay with Grandma Betty. At least there I know I wouldn't be in the way, and she would gladly let me do simple housework, but she and Mike just bought a little one-bedroom house together, and their teenage behavior tells me that sleeping on their couch for the next two months is not even an option.

Again, I'm happy for them, but no thank you.

"Are you coming over for dinner tonight?" she asks.

"Yes. I will be there."

She hugs me tighter.

"I love it when you are home."

Home.

She speaks the word so freely, but it feels foreign to me.

I know what it means, but I can't say that I agree with her.

Lovers is her home. It's been home for Tobias and Natalie for more than a year now, but I don't have a home. I travel so much that I don't see the point in setting roots down anywhere. I'm very aware that owning a house and calling a place home isn't exactly the same thing, but if I owned a house, I wouldn't be there enough to take care of it, and as far as the place I feel most at home … I'm not sure where that is.

I'm just … I'm looking for something, but I have no idea what it is.

I hug Grandma Betty and then follow her to the kitchen. She hugs Tobias and quietly slips out the back door.

"Can I get you anything?" I ask my brother.

He shakes his head. "No. I just need to finish the dishes, and then I'm going to walk into town to get Natalie some of those lemon bars she loves from B's Bakery and maybe even a coffee. One of those white mocha drinks, I think."

"I'll do it," I say with more eagerness than I expected.

"No, I can—"

"I'll do it." I glare at him. "It's just a treat and coffee. I won't mess it up, Tobias."

He takes a breath and nods.

I swear, even though I'm a grown woman, my brother looks at me as if I'm the six-year-old little girl carrying his full glass of milk to the kitchen table and then spilling all over his grilled cheese.

"Thank you."

"It's my pleasure." I grab my purse from their little entrance table and dart out the door.

Finally, I feel like I'm doing something. Like I said, it's just treats and coffee, but it's *something*.

Grandma Betty has lived in Lovers long enough now that I know this town like the back of my hand.

I take my time walking so that I can enjoy how green this place gets during the summer months. I love the big trees that line the streets and tower over the houses and the fact that planting flowers in the front yard is basically a requirement. This place could be the backdrop for a Christmas movie in the winter and a great romantic comedy in the summer.

I pass Mrs. Whitaker's house on the corner of my brother's

street and shake my head at her flower beds and white picket fence. She's outside sweeping the sidewalk to her house. She spots me and waves, so I wave back but don't stop. I might want to take my time to enjoy this place, but I also know that those babies won't let Natalie nap for long.

I cross the street and slow my steps as I near Restore and Repair, Miles Asher's mechanic shop.

He's a *local* local. Some people have moved here and never left, but he's part of one of the families where he was born and raised here and never left.

I know that he worked for the previous owner of the shop before he bought it and renamed it. I know that he's a twin. I know he's about six years older than me. I know his older brother used to play professional hockey. I know he's like a walking piece of art. I swear I've never seen someone more beautiful than Miles. He's very gifted at his craft, loves his family, and I know that he does not like me—not one single bit.

Something I didn't know was that his house is finally done. Last summer, he was still putting finishing touches to it, but wow. That wraparound porch is just screaming at me to grab a book and a tea and relax.

Oh my gosh, and look at the porch swing.

I pull my phone from my purse to take a picture, but then I pause.

Another fact I know about Miles Asher is that, despite me knowing all these things about him, his life is very private, completely the opposite of mine.

I don't know if it's a Miles thing or a small-town thing, but I'm not lying when I say that being back in Lovers over the summer is a breath of fresh air. I don't have to post as much, and I don't question whether every move I make needs to be online for this brand or that one. In fact, in every contract I've signed, I add in a clause that gives me June and July free from work. It's my only guaranteed vacation.

I put my phone back and settle for the mental image of his picture-perfect house instead.

I continue to the bakery, thinking about how my life is so different from those who live here.

When I was in junior high, my parents decided I was old enough to travel with them. That's been their passion since they were young, and they stopped so that they could have kids, but they couldn't shake the itch. So, it was time to get back to it.

Tobias stayed with Grandma to finish school with his friends, but I went with our parents. By the time I could drive, I'd been to more countries than I could count. Once, Mom and Dad were telling someone about our time in Italy, and I'd forgotten about the little town we went to. I forgot. That's how many places I've been.

Traveling so much also meant that I didn't have many friends, so I started a social media page to document my travels and stay connected to all the people I'd met. Now, I have more than a million followers, so snapping pictures and sharing my day-to-day activities feels natural to me.

Don't ask me who my best friend is, though. I'd have to say my brother, Natalie, or my grandmother. I love them, but sometimes you need a friend who isn't blood, and I don't have that. Yeah, I have friends who invite me to travel places with them, but none of them reach out randomly to talk or ask about my day or about my family. Honestly, half of them probably don't even know I have a brother.

I could make up an entire life and no one would know if I was lying.

Which I did once.

I laugh as I remember that day on the beach last summer and then I laugh harder at the idea of me and Miles Asher dating.

I reach the bakery and can basically drool on command at how amazing it smells when I walk inside.

"Quinn!" Sadie Collins calls out after I walk in. "I heard you were back, but I hadn't seen you yet."

She rushes over to give me a hug. Brooke is right behind her.

"I can't believe it's already been a year."

"I was at the signing the other day with my brother and Simon," I tell her. "I wasn't there long, though. Jet leg always gets me, but I agree. The fact that it's been an entire year blows me away."

No matter how long or short my visits are, Brooke and Sadie always make me feel as though we have been friends since the day we were born.

Aside from my family, these two would actually be my next choice for a bestie.

I think that's one of the top things I love about small towns. Well, this one in particular. The people, even though they might not love having tourists all year round, will always treat you like family.

Unless, of course, your name happens to be Miles Asher.

"What brings you into the bakery this afternoon? Normally, I see you only in the mornings." Brooke cocks her hip to the counter and crosses her arms as she waits for my answer.

I let out a long breath.

"Turns out babies know how to party harder than a group of twenty-somethings on vacation in Prague. Those two can pull an all-nighter like it's nobody's business."

Both women chuckle.

"Are you staying with your brother all summer?"

I nod.

"Yep, I'm here for a solid eight weeks this time around."

Grandma Betty loves it, not to mention the little ceremony

she and Mike are having now that they are engaged. They want to keep it small, and I'm thrilled to be here for it.

"Can you go back and forth between their place and your grandmother's?" Sadie asks.

I scrunch my face. "That's not an option."

"Why not?" Brooke asks.

"Because she is my grandmother and I'd like to forever only see her that way. Call me childish; I don't even care. Plus, she and Mike are in a special time of their lives—they don't need some twenty-five-year-old crashing on their couch."

Brooke hands me a coffee, and I hold up two more fingers. "I'm getting drinks and snacks for Tobias and Natalie, too. I also need a half dozen lemon bars."

"You got it," she says, and she starts to box them up, but I do catch the glance she sends Sadie.

Sadie smiles. "I might know of a room you could stay in for the summer if you're interested."

"I'm interested," I say quickly. "Grandma Betty is in love, and Tobias and Natalie are starting to get into a routine, and I'm in the way."

"All right, but you might change your mind once I tell you where the space is."

"Does it have a room?"

Sadie nods.

"A shower?"

She nods again.

"A kitchen and space for me to read?"

She keeps nodding, but now it's her turn to scrunch up her nose.

"I don't see the problem then. I'll take it."

"Well," Sadie draws out as I hand over my credit card to Brooke. "Miles would be your landlord."

Shit.

"Sadie, if you knew that detail, why would you even bring it up?" Brooke asks.

I glance between the two best friends. They are both aware that Miles doesn't care for me, but just like me, they also have no idea why.

Sadie shrugs. "Because Quinn isn't going anywhere, and he needs to suck it up, so I don't think it can hurt to ask him about it. But I also wanted her to be ready just in case he tells her no when she asks about it."

"Thank you for the recommendation, but I have a higher chance of the twins magically sleeping through the night and waking up with no tears."

Brooke snorts.

"Well, it's something to consider if you change your mind."

"Thank you," I tell her and promise to see them later this week.

The walk back to my brother's house is a lot quicker than it was to the bakery. Probably because I want to be sure that I get back before Natalie wakes up.

But I hear crying as I walk up to the front door. I did not make it in time.

Tobias is running around the house like a madman. I take the treats and coffee into the kitchen.

"I'll just put them on a plate for you," I say, but he grabs the box.

"Not needed. Thank you. I'm sorry, I wish I could hang out with you, but why don't you go out and do something? We will see you at dinner, if we make it." He moves around the kitchen quickly, grabbing paper towels and bottles and a few other random things. Then he's headed up the stairs.

I stand here, feeling like I'm in the way again, and not sure what to do next.

I absolutely hate this feeling.

With my purse still slung across my body, I head for the front door.

I want to be one less thing for my brother to worry about, so it looks like I'm going to suck it up and find Miles Asher.

Wish me luck.

CHAPTER THREE

MILES

My favorite part of owning my business is setting my schedule and working at my own pace. I'm efficient, and I like to work quickly, but I make it known that I won't rush a job to meet someone else's deadline, and I won't cut corners. Ever. I won't find a temporary fix. I'll step back, look at the big picture, and pinpoint the problem. Then, I'll find the most effective solution.

Maybe that's why I've never been big on paying for advertising or having social media. My schedule is booked for the remainder of the year and into the new one. Hearing someone's plans to make over a car excites me, so I'd take the job even if I didn't have time for it.

Which is also the reason I've put so much more on my schedule than I can actually do.

I need to hire someone. Quick.

My brothers hound me about being all work and no play, but I don't agree. I have plenty of things I enjoy. I like to read thrillers, thanks to Hudson and his addiction to books growing up. I like to work out. Lately, that's the only time I get to spend with Luca. I like to grill and try new recipes, mixing seasonings together. I like fixing things, which I think stems from my joy in problem-solving. Hence, my job is all about fixing things. Fixing things for other people, anyway. Doing things for myself is a different story. I also enjoy walking out of my three-door shop, just like I am right now, to soak up the sun and watch the people of Lovers mill around living their—shit. *Shit.*

I jump back into the shop, crouching down as I round the front of my current project. I slowly peek over the hood.

Bright red hair flashes across the street.

I drop my chin and let out a breath.

Part of me really did hope she would get the message or at least not show up to my shop this year.

I should have known I wouldn't get that lucky.

I peek again and see her disappear down the street.

Maybe the fact that I wasn't her first stop is a good sign.

Maybe she decided—

"What are you doing down there?"

I jump, falling back onto my ass and hitting the toolbox behind me with my head.

"Oh, sorry! I didn't mean to startle you. I just couldn't find you, and I wasn't sure if you were here or not."

"I'm fine," I snap.

I maneuver to my knees, letting my gaze discreetly take in the long, smooth, lean legs in front of me. From the bright red toes peeking out of her white strappy sandals all the way up to her blue cotton shorts and the orange shirt that reads Sunshine Mixed with Lightning.

But after I stand up fully and my gaze meets hers, I scold myself for being so observant of the woman standing in front of me.

Quinn Banks.

I should have known it was her.

I'm not proud of this admission, but every June, as soon as

she reappears in town, those legs become the subject of my thoughts more than they should be.

She smiles, and I hate that it's genuine.

I hate that every summer she has been here, I've made it clear I don't care to engage in conversation with her, and yet she isn't daunted that I'm a dick to her.

Shit, maybe I'm not great at communication. I have one woman who won't stop texting me and one who pretends I'm not a jerk to her.

Perhaps I need to be clearer with my delivery.

"You're not talking. Are you sure you're all right?" she asks.

"I'm fine. I'm just trying to figure out why you're standing in my shop right now. I didn't invite you here, and as far as I know, you don't own a car that would need to be repaired."

That was pretty clear.

She nods slowly, smirking.

"No, you didn't, and no, I do not. I'm actually here for another reason."

I raise one brow. She should go on, because I won't ask her what it is.

"I heard you had an apartment in the—"

"No."

"But you don't even know what I'm going to say," she argues as I walk past her to the office. It's small, but it's just big enough for a filing cabinet, a desk, and two chairs. Office work is my least favorite part of this business, as I've mentioned, so I like to keep it simple. The stack of paperwork on the chair behind the desk, though, is not so simple.

"I don't need to," I say. "You can go."

"Well, I heard that you—"

"I said no."

"Can I at least give you my speech? You might change your mind."

"Doubtful."

My gaze flickers to her legs, slowly moving up her body to her small waist and full chest. Everything about her screams my type. It has since the first day I laid eyes on her years ago.

"Miles, please," she says softly. My name rolls off her tongue as if she's begging. Pleading. It makes my heart pound quickly.

I let out a huff.

I don't care much for that either.

I'm not blind, all right. I'm aware that I checked her out when she walked up. I'm aware that my body is attracted to her every single time she steps back into this town. I'm aware that, given different circumstances, I'd be asking her out and attempting to get to know her as more than friends or acquaintances or whatever you want to call it.

But that is not what's happening here.

What's happening is she obviously needs a place to stay for the summer, and I've already decided that the apartment is not going to be a tourist destination.

"I don't rent to tourists," I say, cutting off any hope she might have of winning me over.

She follows me into my office.

I move the stack of papers and sit behind the desk, leaning back in the chair.

Quinn crosses her arms and cocks her hip.

"I wouldn't exactly call myself a tourist at this point."

"Do you live here permanently?" I ask.

She narrows her eyes. "No."

"Do you own a business here?"

"No."

"Do you own anything here?"

She rolls her eyes at that one.

"No."

"Then, by definition, you are a tourist."

"What dictionary is that from? Miles Asher is a pompous prick?"

Ah, so she can read a room.

"Is that your way of convincing me to say yes?"

"Maybe. Is it working?"

"No."

"Tell me the real reason you won't rent to me. You know my grandmother and my brother. My family lives here, works here, and *owns* more than one business here. That has to count for something, right?"

I twist my lips as I think over her response.

"Maybe it means I'm half local," she adds quickly.

"That's not a thing. I said no. Now, if you don't mind, I have work to do."

I get up and walk right past her, back to the garage.

I was convinced that walking into my office would make her think I was busy, but that didn't work. So here I am, actually getting to work to make her go away.

I glance at her as she steps out of the office and heads out of the garage. But she stops, turns, and faces me over the two cars between us. I stand a little taller, waiting to hear her final argument.

"Why don't you like me?" she asks. Her voice is smooth and without emotion. She's not asking because she's sad or mad that I refused to let her rent my apartment. No, she's asking out of pure curiosity. It's the first time in years she's come right out and asked me about it, so it takes me by surprise.

I let out a small laugh and shake my head.

"Haven't you figured that out yet?"

"Obviously not if I'm asking you."

Touché.

"People like you come to this town, take what they want for however long they want it, and then they leave with no consideration for the people they are leaving behind. So no, I don't want to rent to someone who couldn't care less about this town and is just looking for something that benefits only them."

Her lips part, but I hold my hand up. "I can keep being a dick, Quinn, or you can walk out that door and accept that, for once, you're not getting your way."

Her head jerks back as if I slapped her.

For a fleeting moment, I see something flash in her eyes.

It's a look I can't describe, and it momentarily makes me feel guilty for being so crass.

Maybe Quinn isn't as unfazed by me as I thought.

She walks away with her head down.

Part of me says I need to apologize, but the other says it's not my problem.

My problem is finding the best way to avoid Cherry and keep my shop up to speed so that I can continue doing what I do best.

Fixing cars and keeping to myself.

CHAPTER FOUR

QUINN

I don't always get my way.

Screw him.

Gah. He barely even let me speak.

He's a dick.

A giant dick.

I'm no stranger to mean people or rude comments. My follower count is evidence of that. People aren't scared to express their feelings online, and I've received more horrid comments about my pictures, my life, my clothes, and my body than I care to admit.

But to my face, that's a different story.

To say I always get my way … that one just hurts.

If I had my way, I'd … I'd … I don't even know.

I hug my laptop closer to my chest and head into B's Bakery for a late afternoon coffee and a snack. As soon as I left Miles's shop, I went back to my brother's, where he, Natalie, and both babies were sleeping in the living room. I quietly grabbed my computer and came here.

I find a table by the front window next to the door. Daisy is working now, and she's kind but not chatty.

Right now, I'm okay with that.

I open my Mac and touch the finger pad to wake it up.

My social media pops up right away to where I left off the last time.

I've been traveling for more than ten years, and I've had this account for just as long. But I'll be honest: it just doesn't hold the spark it once did for me.

I still love traveling. Don't mistake that part, but something is missing.

Society tells me that it's because everyone around me is either meeting someone, engaged, getting married, or having babies and that I need that, too.

But I'm not so convinced. At the same time, I have no idea what's missing.

Am I lonely? Am I bored? Am I just being picky? Am I overthinking?

I stare at the photo on the screen.

It's me, with London Bridge in the background. I'm smiling, but the longer I stare at it, the more I think … is that even my real smile?

Ugh.

Miles did this. He got in my head, and now I'm sitting here letting my mind run wild.

The door to the bakery's kitchen opens, and Sadie steps out with Hudson.

She might not own this place anymore, but she is here enough to make everyone wonder.

"I'm just saying. There has to be a way for him to get the message through that he isn't interested in her."

"She's clueless," Hudson says, placing his hand on Sadie's lower back as they walk toward the front door of the bakery.

"Hi, Quinn." Sadie smiles and pauses at my table. "I'm sorry that Miles didn't go for the rental thing with the apartment."

That was like a half hour ago.

That's small-town life for you. News always travels quickly.

"It's fine." I wave my hand in front of my face and then close my computer. "I'll be fine at my brother's. Just expect to see me multiple times a day for coffee."

Oh god, is this what I'm going to do every single day of the summer?

Come to the coffee shop?

"Is everything okay?" Sadie asks. "You looked like you zoned out there for a moment."

"I'm good," I say with my best smile.

Sadie's bottom lip sticks out. "I wish I knew the answer for whatever you need, too."

"Me too?" I ask. "Who else needs help?"

Maybe if I can hear about someone else's problems, I can focus on that instead of my own life.

"Miles," she answers quickly.

"He'll be fine, Sadie," Hudson says, rubbing her back.

"No, he won't. We aren't going to see him all summer if Cherry keeps this up. He'll hide in his shop every single day."

The image of Miles behind the front of that car comes to mind.

"Who's Cherry?"

"This girl who is obsessed with Miles. No matter how many times he turns her down, she seems to think she still has a chance. Heck, Hudson, do we need to find him a girlfriend? Maybe if Cherry sees him with someone, she will back off."

"Miles isn't exactly the dating type. Besides, if we help him do anything, it's find him some office help. He won't admit it, but he's behind." His phone rings. "Shoot, I need to take this call," Hudson says as he walks out the door.

Like before, Sadie sticks her bottom lip out.

Maybe if I offer to help Miles with his office stuff, he'll be more open to renting me the apartment.

I'm two seconds away from asking Sadie more about what Miles needs when the door to the bakery opens, and my heart basically thumps its way into my throat.

"Oh my gosh, this place is adorable."

"How cute is this?"

"Fuck, this place smells good."

Sadie steps back as Andy, Sully, and Ashley spill into B's Bakery.

I'm half tempted to slap myself.

Is this real?

"Quinny!" Andy yells as soon as she spots me. "I was hoping I'd run into you."

I stand slowly as she comes around the table to hug me.

It's real. It's very real.

The shock continues to settle in.

"This town is just as cute as you described it. When Sully and I were looking up venues for the wedding and found Lovers Lodge, I knew it was meant to be."

"And then we talked about how much you love this place, and we knew you wouldn't ever steer someone wrong, so here we are," Ashley says, now standing next to Andy. "For the summer."

"The summer," I repeat, finally finding my words.

"Yep. This will be one of our best vacations yet." Sully grins and then rests his arm around Andy's shoulders.

"I'm sorry to interrupt,"—Sadie waves a hand—"I'm heading out. I wish there was more I could do to help you. Do you want me to talk to Miles? Maybe that will help."

"Miles?" Ashley jumps into the conversation. "*The* Miles?"

Oh my god. Kill me. Kill me now.

"Your boyfriend lives here? In Lovers." Andy is grinning. "And you know him?" she asks Sadie.

"I … yes," she responds.

I want to crawl into a hole and disappear.

"Well, don't let me keep you, Sadie," I say and rush around the table, hug her, and walk her to the door, where I whisper, "Please pretend you didn't hear that. I'll tell you about it later."

She nods and waves goodbye. Hudson is outside waiting for her.

"This is great. We can all hang out, and Quinny won't be the odd wheel anymore. And we have the entire summer. Oh, I'm so excited." Andy beams.

Please, someone put me out of my misery. Please.

"When can we meet him?" Sully asks. "You know my brother is going to be devastated when I tell him that Miles lives here. I think he was hoping to rekindle what you had a couple of summers ago."

Oh hell, this just keeps getting worse.

"Well, you know," I start and then begin to collect my things so I can leave this situation immediately. "He works a lot, so I'm not sure that he will have a lot of extra time."

"So when do you see him?"

"Me?"

"Yeah. If he works so much," Ashley asks.

"Well, I mean, he makes time for me."

"Oh, that's good."

"I'm actually off to see him now, but you can all text or message me or whatever, and we can plan something, but I really have to be going. So happy to see you." I dash out the door.

Before I can change my mind. I walk briskly toward Restore and Repair.

I have no idea what I'm going to say or do, but I know there will be begging. Lots of it.

I could turn around right now and tell them we broke up, but they are here for the whole summer. One of them is bound to run into Miles or Luca or even Hudson, and people talk. They'd eventually find out I lied.

I lied about being in a relationship.

How sad is that?

Not as sad as what I'm about to do.

As soon as I reach the shop, I see a redhead hovering outside the three garage doors.

Is this Cherry? I don't want to be judgmental because I hate that, but honestly, it would make sense with her bright red hair.

I slow my steps. She seems fidgety as she rises and lowers from the tips of her toes to her heels, peeking into the shop as if she were looking for someone.

If she can't find him, then he must not be there.

Unless …

I reroute my steps and head to the side of the building. Then I help myself to the back door and walk in as if I own the place. As soon as I crack the door from the back office to the garage, I see him sitting in the corner on the floor behind one of the cars.

Each shoulder touches a wall, his legs criss-crossed in front of him and his computer on his lap. I glance out the big doors; Cherry is still lurking.

This is it. This is how I'll convince him to rent to me. We both need this.

Slowly, because I'm unsure what Cherry can and can't see inside the shop, I crouch to Miles's level. I open the door just a sliver more so he can see me. There is no way I can open the door entirely without drawing her attention, though, so I'll have to talk with him from here.

"Miles," I whisper rather loudly.

He startles, his hands doing this weird shake that causes them to hit his computer screen. He barely catches it before it falls off his lap.

For the first time in my life, I understand exactly what the phrase "if looks could kill" means.

I try not to smile at his glare.

"What the hell are you doing?" he whispers back.

"Well, I came to talk to you about the apartment."

"Jesus. Can nobody take a hint? I said no, Quinn. I do not have time for this."

I nod slowly. I hear him. I should probably just apologize and leave, because it's clear he doesn't want to talk to me. However, if he had to pick between me and Cherry, I think maybe I stand a chance at being his first choice.

Maybe.

I think.

"I know, but I have an idea that helps you."

"For fuck's sake," he mumbles and goes back to his computer.

"I see you're working hard, but I imagine you'd like to get back to the hands-on stuff."

He ignores me.

"And I have the feeling that you're only doing the computer side of the business right now because of the redhead standing outside the doors."

Still, he won't look up, but he does close his eyes and take a deep breath.

"I can make her go away."

His attention snaps to me. His eyes narrow like always, but instead of asking me for more information, he just goes back to whatever is on his screen.

"For the entire summer."

I see the moment his jaw clenches from grinding his teeth.

Like before, he closes his eyes for a split moment before locking them on mine.

I've never noticed how blue they are until right now.

Miles has really pretty eyes. They remind me of the ocean.

"I'm going to regret asking this, but how?"

"First, I need you to agree that if my plan is good, I get to rent the apartment for the next eight weeks."

"No."

"Fine. Enjoy your summer with Cherry." I start to stand.

"Wait," he whispers-shouts. "Fuck. Fine. This better be good."

"It's great. You tell her I'm your girlfriend."

He snorts. "Yeah, sure, and poof, she's gone, huh?"

I nod.

"If me telling her that I'm not interested isn't going to work, what makes you think she's going to believe we are suddenly dating and accept it?"

"We won't know for sure until we find out."

"I'd rather take my chances doing anything else. No thanks."

"Oh my god, do you ever just stop and listen to anyone?"

"Yeah. Plenty of times."

"When?"

He smirks

"In bed."

I blink once, twice, but I can't think of anything and now my mind is trying to imagine him in—

"You're trying to picture it, aren't you?"

"No," I defend myself. "No."

I totally was. I mean, come on, he's a mechanic. Forget his listening skills; one would have to assume he's good with his hands, right?

He chuckles, and the sound practically tickles my skin, causing goose bumps to cover my body.

"Too bad. Sounds like something you'd like to see. Anyway, like I said, I'll take my chances doing something else."

I don't have that same mindset, and even though I'm confused on how to feel about everything he just said, I'm not willing to take the chance of him saying no. I need this right now, and if I can get it without having to tell him all the details of why I need him to agree, I'm taking it.

"Looks like that's been working out super well for you," I snap, changing the subject "Do most mechanics sit on the floor when they work?"

"As a matter of fact, we do spend time down here."

"Hiding?"

"I'm not hiding."

"You're definitely hiding."

"No, I'm not."

"Fine. Then stop whispering."

"Hell, you're annoying."

"And you're infuriating, but we must move on."

"I'm not fake dating you, Quinn."

"If I can get her to leave in less than five minutes, we will fake a date and you'll rent to me."

"Holy fuck, you're relentless."

"I'm desperate, Miles." In so, so many ways. "I'm physically sitting on the floor of an office, asking the man who despises me more than anything in the world to pretend to date me just so I can rent an apartment. Please, Miles."

I swear his face wrinkles in pain.

"Please."

"Five minutes, but that's it."

I barely let him finish before I scoot back and head back out the way I came in.

I'm not messing up this chance by waiting a moment longer. I need this more than he does.

Shit, maybe I am a little selfish.

I step outside, take a glance to my right at the door that leads to the apartment, and then I round the building to the front. I adjust my purse, then I step into Cherry's view.

"Oh, hi," I say and stop. "Can I help you?"

She shakes her head.

"Nope. I'm just waiting for Miles to get back."

"Oh, let me go find him for you."

"He doesn't like people walking into his shop if he doesn't know they are here." Cherry jumps in front of me. "And I was here first."

I give her my best smile and shake my head. "That is so Miles. I don't think he'll be upset if it's me, though. It would be silly for him to be upset with his girlfriend for showing up to see him."

I try to move past her, but she stops me again.

"His what?"

"His girlfriend." I offer her my hand. "Hi, I'm Quinn Banks."

Her eyes widen, and then she stumbles back like I hit her.

"I didn't know he was seeing someone. Weirdly, he never mentioned it, but I *have* heard your name before."

"Oh, well, he's pretty private," I say, ignoring how she might know me. "Do you want me to tell him you stopped by?"

"Um, no. That's okay."

Yet she doesn't leave. I fight the urge to look at my phone. Not that I'll know if it's been five minutes or not. I didn't look when I left the office.

I open my mouth to ask her if she's all right because, honestly, I can see by the way her shoulders drop that this is not what she wants to hear, but she finally storms away from the shop.

A part of me feels a little bad, but a bigger part of me is relieved as I return to find Miles.

"She's gone."

Miles stands slowly.

He lets out a deep breath.

"That took six minutes."

"Oh my god, are you being serious? I saved your butt just now. She would have stayed all night."

"I know." He shrugs off his plaid jacket, leaving himself in just a white T-shirt that reveals his thick and sculpted arms. He runs a hand through his thick brown hair and sighs. Then he grabs a rag from the toolbox in the corner, folds it, and tucks it into the back pocket of his blue jeans before leaning into the hood of a vehicle.

He's not going to give me the apartment or fake date me. I'm going to look like a fool. Which serves me right, but a little compassion right now would be nice.

I could argue or stomp my foot like a child, but it's clear that nothing will work.

I turn just as he says. "How do we convince the rest of the town?"

"What?"

He stands taller and crosses his arms. "People are aware of the way you and I normally interact. They won't buy it if we start showing up all touchy and shit."

He's right.

"I didn't think that far ahead," I admit.

"We've never gotten along," he says as a fact.

"I know."

"But then I let you rent the apartment behind my shop."

My face lights up.

"And the more times we saw each other—" he says.

"—the more we developed an affection for the other," I finish for him. "It also helps that you've been slowly hitting on me for years and now you hired me to get caught up on your books and whatever."

"Jesus, now I have to hire you, too? What else do you want, the pin number to my bank accounts?"

I cross my arms and smile. "I have my own money, but thank you for asking."

He rolls his eyes.

"Come on, Miles. You need the help, and I have time to spare for the next eight weeks. After that, I'm gone and out of your hair—office and apartment. I'll even let you be the one to break us up."

He takes a deep breath.

Please say yes. Please. Please.

"It'll have to work for now, but we don't tell anyone the truth, got it? Luca is my best friend, but Hudson and I didn't call him Loose Lips Luca for no reason growing up. And we only do this until I can think of a better way to get through to Cherry."

I can't help but smile.

I didn't have to get him into bed for him to listen long enough to agree.

This also might be the first time Miles has ever told me anything about his actual life.

So it's probably not the best time to tell him that, after what she's heard, Sadie will definitely know this isn't real.

"Okay, that's a smart idea," I reply anyway. "Have you done this before?"

Miles gives me a look that screams *are you fucking kidding me right now?*

"Yeah, Quinn, I fake date women all the time. Last month, I fake dated this girl who wanted new tires."

I cross my arms and glare at him.

Oh my, that's some thick sarcasm. Well, it's like sarcasm mixed with a joke. Maybe.

Does Miles know how to be funny?

"Please don't be a dick," I settle with.

"Don't ask stupid questions."

"Are we going to be able to do this? We can't even have a conversation without fighting."

"No, we can't, but as much as I don't want to admit it"—he blows out a breath—"I think this might work to get Cherry to back off for good, so we need to figure it out."

"We could start by you showing me the apartment."

He yanks the towel from his back pocket and tosses it onto the counter in front of him.

"If this allows me to finally return to work in peace, let's do it."

He passes by me, and I think it's the first time he isn't scowling at me.

I follow him out the back and to the apartment door.

"I usually get to work around five, so don't be alarmed if you hear me early in the morning. The shop door can get sticky in the top corner and makes a popping noise. I'll fix it by the end of the summer."

"Okay."

He unlocks the door then peels the key off the key ring he'd grabbed on the way out the shop.

"I don't have a spare, so don't lose this."

"Got it."

Finally, he steps inside, and there is no hiding the shock on my face.

The space is bright thanks to white walls, trim, and open windows. The living room, dining room, and kitchen are all one big room. The bedroom is straight back to the right, and the bathroom next to it. The entire apartment is fully furnished with soft blues and yellows, and even though it's small, it's absolutely perfect.

Miles moves to the other side of the living room and pulls back a curtain.

I almost gasp at the sliding door to a deck just big enough for the table, two chairs, and a porch swing that matches the one at his house. There isn't a railing, but there are exactly three steps that lead down to the grass. Directly across from the deck is Mile's front porch. And behind his house is Lovers Lake with a backdrop of the mountain.

"Wow," I say. I already knew I loved his house, but now I'll see it every morning when I wake up, along with the view behind it.

He grips the back of his neck. "We built it like this so my dad could easily walk to my place without going around the entire shop. Not in a creepy way for me to watch whoever lives here."

"It's beautiful, Miles. Thank you."

He nods and starts to leave.

"Wait, did we establish that I'm working for you, too? Or rent? What do you need me to sign?"

He lets out another breath, and I'm starting to catch on to the fact that he does this as he thinks over his next words.

"This is Lovers, Quinn. I said I'm going to rent to you for the next eight weeks, and I'll keep my word. We don't need a contract. Rent is free because you'll be working for me. Do you even know how to do anything in an office?"

"I do. Do you want me to send you a resumé?" I swing my bag around and begin to open it to pull out my computer. "I just need to hook my laptop up to your printer. Can it go wireless?"

His left brow peaks as he stares at me.

"Do you have a printer?" I ask.

"Yes."

"Okay, can I—"

"The job starts tomorrow at seven. Do not be late."

"Thank you!"

I move to hug him, my arms up and slowly opening, but he sidesteps so quickly that I stumble.

He grabs my arm to steady me.

"You're welcome," he says quickly and walks right out the door.

Miles Asher. Not a hugger. Got it.

But he is my new boss *and* my new boyfriend.

The smile on my lips starts to fade as that statement settles in my mind and relief floods my body.

But of course, then reality sets in.

Oh, crap.

I'm going to need some luck.

A lot of it.

CHAPTER FIVE

MILES

Seeing the light on outside the shop apartment as soon as I walked out my front door this morning was like a slap in the face for every poor choice I made yesterday.

I made bad choices to take care of other bad choices.

I'm in my thirties. I should know better by now.

Fuck.

I'm fake dating Quinn Banks to keep Cherry away from me.

What kind of person does that?

Me. Apparently.

Is it a stupid plan? Yes.

Am I smarter than this? Yes.

Is this going to end in disaster? Yes, probably.

But am I also desperate? Extremely.

About four years ago, Cherry's father came into my shop because he drove over a nail during a scenic mountain drive. He noticed the Mustang that was in the shop and asked me question after question about it. After an hour or so, I had him on my books for three different cars. The next day, he brought a friend to meet me—another booking. The next week, he brought me two friends. More bookings.

The amount of people those friends have brought me is incredible.

He could have booked his cars and just left it at that. But he clearly liked my work, and because of that, I owe a lot of my success to him.

Which is exactly why I can't tell his daughter to just fuck off, as much as I want to. I tried the "I think we should be friends" and the "I don't have feelings for you like that" and the "you deserve better than someone like me" and that straightforward "no, thank you."

None of it has worked.

But me dating someone, even if it's not real—well, it might actually work.

Still, I have got to figure something out. There's no way Quinn and I are going to be able to pull this off.

My family, for starters, is going to be suspicious from the first time they see us together. However we do this, we need to do it right. I don't want to look like a fool, and right now, I'm feeling a little like one for even going along with this.

But as I saw yesterday, a fake relationship does what I need it to do, so I'm giving it a shot.

I unlock the shop door and jerk it open, cursing when it sticks in the corner again.

I flip the lights on and walk right through the office to the shop. Apparently, Quinn is going to handle all of that now.

I let out a deep sigh.

Don't even get me started on that whole thing. I only know her as someone who travels, takes pictures, and shares them for the world to see. I'm also aware that she shares different products for different companies online, but again, I have no clue how that is going to help her with the office shit I need her to do for me. Although, she sounded confident enough.

Fuck.

Did I really hire someone because she sounds confident?

I'm so in over my head here.

"Morning!" Quinn says right behind me, and I startle, spinning around to face her. As soon as I gather myself, I point at her.

"Rule fucking one, stop scaring me."

She sighs and crosses her arms in front of her.

"I wouldn't scare you if you weren't so paranoid. Seriously? What's your deal?"

Instead of answering, I point over her shoulder.

"You work in there, and I work out here."

She nods. "Got it, straight to business—that's fine, but maybe you can at least come show me exactly what you want me to do and where you left off."

She's right, but there's no way in hell I'm going to tell her that.

I walk past her, and she follows me.

"Sit," I say and pull out the chair behind the desk.

She grins.

"A man who gives orders. I could get on board with that."

Jesus.

"As your boss, it looks like you lucked out."

"My boss and my *boyfriend*. Wow. We move fast."

"Can you be serious?" I ask, moving to stand behind her so I can show her what to do on the computer. "This is my job. This is how I pay my bills."

"Yes, I can," she answers as she turns on the computer. "Sorry. I was just trying to make light of our situation, but clearly that is not the right move. I won't do it again. So, what programs do you use? QuickBooks, NetSuite, maybe even Quicken. Personally, I think Quicken is a bit outdated, so I haven't used it for a while, but I could get by. For what you've got going on here, between the labor hours and parts and materials, I think QuickBooks would be the best. But again, as I said, I can work with whatever you have."

Zero. Words.

Labor hours? Parts? Materials? It's all generic to what I'd have on an invoice, but everything just fell out of her mouth as if she's said it a hundred times.

"You're shocked. I get it. Most people are when I talk about anything other than traveling and which suitcase is best for a weekend getaway."

"I'm not shocked," I say quickly, even though I sure as hell am. "I just …"

"It's fine, really. So, what software do you use?"

I scratch my neck and grab my little notebook with passwords in it, handing it to her so she can log into the computer.

"Excel."

She logs in without a word and then spins to face me. "Like for …"

Our eyes linger, waiting for the other to speak first.

"For …" She continues to wait for me to say… what? I don't understand exactly what she's asking.

"Everything."

"Miles, seriously? You can't use it for everything. You have a thriving business and need to be tracking this better. How long have you been using just spreadsheets? How far behind on billing are you? What's your inventory like? What about payroll? How do you do that with a spreadsheet?"

Her questions blur together. I just make it work. It feels like a mess when I do it, but I get it done, and so far the guy who does my taxes hasn't told me I'm doing anything wrong.

But now, I'm starting to think that perhaps hiring Quinn might not be as foolish as I thought it would just minutes ago.

"Here." I open a drawer. "These are the invoices I'm behind on. You can use my spreadsheet; there is a folder on the desktop. It sounds like you'll find it easily. You can use that to get started, or you can buy one of those fancy programs you just mentioned."

She simply nods as she starts to go through the notebook that has my chicken scratch for billing on it. I'm possibly three, maybe four months behind.

I know. I know.

I wasn't kidding when I said that I liked the hands-on side of this job better.

"I trust you to pick a good one."

That statement gets her attention.

"Wow. Okay. I'll get started on this right away, but I do think we need to set some ground rules. Especially for the dating part. We are about to spend a lot of time together, and we don't want to mess this up."

"I agree. We can go over it when we eat lunch. I need to get to work."

"Okay."

I turn to leave.

"Wait!" Quinn calls out.

"What are these?"

I glance over my shoulder to see she's pointing to the sticky notes lined across the top of the desk with dates and names on them.

"That's my schedule."

Her eyes grow wide.

"Maybe you can organize that, too?"

"Oh, I will. This is—"

I walk out the door before she can finish.

As I make my way to the vehicle that's going to steal my attention for the next few hours, I can't help but smile.

Who would have thought that hiring Quinn was going to be a good thing?

Not me.

Forget the Cherry part of this deal—if fake dating her gets my business caught up, I'm on board.

I better not fuck this up.

———

"Miles!"

I pop my head out from under the Chevy and find Quinn looking at me. Her arms are crossed over her tank top and sweater jacket thing. She looks annoyed, but I don't focus too much on that because her bare legs have every ounce of my attention.

Why am I obsessed with her legs?

Am I a leg man and didn't know it?

Maybe I should tell her that longer shorts are the dress code here.

"What?" I snap.

This might be the first time she's interrupted me today, but seeing as how I've always worked alone, it annoys me that someone is interrupting me at all.

She rolls her emerald eyes and then narrows them at me.

"It's almost two. Have you eaten?"

Oh, look, it's me being a dick again, and she's being nice.

"No."

"Do you want me to go get something, or do you want to take a break?"

"I can't take a break right now."

"You can take a break."

"No, I need to work, Quinn."

"And you need to eat, Miles. Plus, we need to set rules before word gets out."

How in the hell would word get out if the two of us haven't told anyone yet?

"Are you going to argue with me until I listen to you?" I ask.

"Yes. You can be the best at this kind of work and still take ten minutes to eat."

I smirk, and just as I'm opening my mouth to comment on her comment, she holds her hand up.

"Don't even start. I complimented you. Let's move on."

I let out a chuckle, but her bored expression remains.

"I'll eat when—"

Before I can finish that sentence, my stomach growls so loudly that Quinn actually steps back.

"Why don't I just go get us something and bring it back?"

"Yeah, maybe that's best," I say.

Quinn turns and starts to walk out of the shop.

She didn't ask what I wanted or where to go.

I'm about to shout that just a burger from Hudson's is great, but she reappears, speed-walking toward me with her head down.

"Cherry is outside."

"What?" I duck as if someone is swinging a bat at my face. "I thought you got rid of her."

"Well, I did my best, and she's not exactly outside the shop, she's just near it, so there is a good chance she's not here to see you. But if I walk out there and you are not with me, she will know that—"

"I'm in here alone. Shit," I finish her ramble.

"Yeah."

I let out a big sigh and then grab my rag from my back pocket and wipe my hands.

"Let me wash up. We can go eat together."

"Great. I'll grab the spreadsheets I printed earlier with the different programs on it, and we can go over them."

Spreadsheets?

I finish at the sink before Quinn reappears, so I head toward the office because, let's be honest, I'm not about to walk outside alone.

I'm not scared of Cherry.

I'm annoyed with the situation I put myself into, and the more she keeps popping up, the more I'm worried that I might say something I'll regret and all that business that comes my way will go poof, bye-bye.

"How many spreadsheets did you—"

I stop dead in my tracks.

My office is … holy shit, it's so clean. I slowly look from one side to the other.

The cabinets are labeled alphabetically, the white chairs that were starting to look light brown are white again, I can see the top of the desk and the little basket things I bought once thinking they'd help me get more organized are stacked with papers in them. Even the dish my nephew Max bought me on my last birthday for my peanut M&M addiction is out of the box and filled with the little chocolate candies.

I pop the lid off and grab a handful as I continue to observe the room.

"When did you buy a plant?" I ask her, pointing to the one in the small window behind the desk, then toss an M&M into my mouth.

"It's from the apartment. I thought I could place one in here to make it a little homier. Also, I saw the pictures you've taken of past projects in one of your computer files, and I think we should get them printed and hang some of them up in here."

I glance from the small plant to Quinn.

"I know that's not what you hired me for, but like I said, your work is good. I think we need to show it."

I don't really know what to say. It's not often I get compliments that aren't from customers, and Quinn just gave me two in the last ten minutes.

I nod, give her a half-ass smile, and then nod to the door. "Let's go eat."

Quinn doesn't move. "You really don't have anything to say back?"

"I do not. Let's go eat."

"I'm sorry, but I need a moment to just … I left Miles Asher speechless. And you didn't argue with me. Wow. Is this a reflection of how you listen in bed? I bet you get laid a lot if so. No wonder this girl is obsessed with—"

"Okay, let's move on and eat," I all but growl.

I do not need to be thinking about how often I get laid—which isn't as often as she's suggesting—and about Quinn at the same time.

Hell, I'm still annoyed with myself for bringing it up yesterday. The way her lips parted, her cheeks flushed, and her gaze darkened had me hard in a matter of seconds.

Talking sex with Quinn needs to always be off-limits.

I touch the small of her back to gently encourage her to get moving.

"I mean this is—"

"Do you ever stop talking? Or can you ever let someone else have the last word?" I cut her off.

"No and no."

I let out a small chuckle as we step out of the shop.

At least she's honest about it.

"Hearing you laugh is not something I'm—"

"Hi," Cherry says, stepping in front of us as soon as we are outside and twisting her fingers together as she glances at Quinn. "I didn't know you'd be here."

"Oh," Quinn says softly. "I'm actually working in the office with Miles now."

"You two are dating and working together?"

The question is clearly directed at Quinn. She nods.

Quickly, Cherry looks at me. "I just wanted to say hi since I hadn't seen you yet this summer and I'm back. Not that it matters now, but yeah, hi."

If there was a time to feel like a dick—well, a bigger dick—it's now.

Cherry is kind, but she's a little clueless when it comes to taking a hint.

"It's good to see you," I tell her, and her face lights up like a fucking Christmas tree at Rockefeller Center. I cringe on the inside.

It's a common remark to the average person, but Cherry is not average.

Quinn elbows me, so I clear my throat.

"We are heading to lunch. I'll see you around."

"You will?" Cherry lights up again, and Quinn practically jerks me forward.

"Bye!" Cherry says with a lot more enthusiasm than when she started our little conversation.

Quinn and I both wave.

"Looks like you have the jealous girlfriend thing down pretty good," I say.

Quinn snorts. "Or maybe she thinks you're into her because of your comments."

"Oh, come on, those are nothing specific to one person. Everyone says them."

"Not to people they are trying to avoid. *Good to see you. See you around.* Those are trigger words for a girl in love with a man who doesn't love her back."

"She's not in love with me," I say as we turn onto Main Street.

"If she's not, she's damn near close. This might be harder than we thought."

"Yeah, maybe we shouldn't do this. It's already complicated enough."

I open the door to Hudson's, and Quinn walks in. I'm right behind her, pointing over her shoulder to the bar. I'm a pretty routine guy, and sitting where I can see the doors is my go-to move. I like to be ready for anything.

It isn't until I rest my hand on the back of her chair, leaning in to make a suggestion for lunch —solely for the purpose that we order, eat, and get back to work—that I see both of my brothers watching me. One two chairs down eating lunch himself and one behind the bar.

This might not have been the best choice for lunch today, but it's too late now.

"What?" I direct the question at Luca and Hudson. Quinn shifts from studying the menu to looking at my brothers, causing her body to brush against mine. From their view, I have no doubt that Quinn and I are looking pretty cozy on this lunch "date."

"Hey, guys," she says in a cheery tone. I'll be completely honest. Before our little arrangement, I wanted to roll my eyes because she's so damn happy all the time, but now I want to do it because, in just the past twenty-four hours, I've learned the voice she's giving them isn't her real one. It's not fake per se, but it definitely screams *I need to be extra cheery because I may or may not be fake dating the guy next to me.*

My fault completely.

Apparently, I'm a bit of a mess.

Of course, it would be Quinn Banks who brings this to my attention.

I wave with two fingers to my brothers, but that's all they get in greeting since neither have yet to say a word.

Quinn nudges me with her elbow again, and I flinch.

"Stop doing that," I say between gritted teeth.

"Stop being weird," she mimics me, keeping a smile on her face.

"What are you two up to?" Luca, who found his words, practically sing-songs as he strolls over. He sits right next to me and props his chin up on one hand as he leans on the bar.

"We are eating lunch, Luca. What does it look like?"

"Well, for starters, it seems like—"

"I'm helping in the shop and renting the apartment behind it," Quinn cuts him off.

It makes me want to smile. She doesn't even live here full time, and she knows my brother well enough to know he was about to just let all his thoughts fall from his lips like a kid with food poisoning. Uncontrolled and way too fucking much.

"Oh," is all Luca says.

"And he invited me to lunch after we spent the morning together."

She gives me a wink.

I'd laugh if I weren't so terrified at how calm she is right now and a little alarmed at the innuendo she clearly just made that leaves my brother speechless.

Instead, I just stare at her.

She takes a breath, clearing her throat and letting her gaze flicker to my hand behind her. It wasn't exactly a natural move, but Luca is too shocked to notice, and Hudson is busy working.

I move my hand from the back of her chair to her back and give her two small strokes.

"See anything you like?"

"Oh, I've always loved the food here." She smiles at me.

Okay, so it might be a little overkill right now, but I don't care. Luca remains silent. I'm going to enjoy that for a little while longer.

"I'll take a bacon cheeseburger with fries and mustard."

I fake gag. "What? Did you mean to say ranch?"

"No."

"Pretty sure you did. Or even maybe ketchup or fry sauce or even barbecue sauce, but you definitely said—"

"Mustard. I know."

"Are you two ready to order?" Hudson asks as he joins us. Then he looks at Luca, who is still stunned, watching Quinn and me. "What happened to him?"

"I'm not sure," I say, quickly followed by "two of the usual but one with mustard."

Even Hudson looks at Quinn with disgust.

He walks off to place our order while Quinn and I pretend Luca isn't here.

"So," she starts and pulls out her folder with the printed spreadsheets. "I looked at three different software programs and put their comparisons here." She hands me the papers. "It's pretty clear which one you'll want to get based on price and what you want out of it."

"Why didn't you just buy one?"

"Because I wanted you to see your options. 'Just buy one'"—she uses fake air quotes on the last three words—"isn't a smart business move."

I raise a brow and look her in the eyes.

She shoves my shoulder.

"Stop. I wasn't insulting you as a businessman, okay. I'm just saying"—she lowers her voice and leans in closer to me—"I know you're significantly thrilled to work with me all day every day, but I'm not going to let your need to quickly get out of my presence hurt your company, even if it is something as silly as buying software."

Who is this woman?

I mean, I know what I see online and what I've seen in short meetings over the time she's visited Lovers, but the way she is talking right now, it's … I don't know, but it bothers me, too.

"Well, I think—"

"Quinn," a deep voice says behind us.

She spins quickly, her knees hitting mine and forcing me to turn with her. We come face-to-face with a man in a suit. He's got his arm around a petite brunette whose eyes grow to the size of saucers as she squeals.

"Quinney! Oh my gosh. Sully here said he saw you, but I was like 'what are the odds that we run into her two days in a row?'"

"Andy." Quinn stands and hugs her. "I'm sorry about yesterday. I was in such a hurry and didn't give you a proper welcome."

Andy keeps squealing while jumping as they hug.

"I'm just so excited that we get to spend the summer in Lovers. It's been one day, and I already love it here. It's so quiet."

"I told my brother that you were here, and he's excited, even if you do have a boyfriend or whatever."

We just decided to fake date yesterday. How do Quinn's friends know already? Did she call them right after I agreed?

"Your brother is here already?" Quinn slowly sits down and her hand falls to my thigh.

I'd be concerned about the move she's making, but I'm too distracted by the way her hand is shaking.

"Yeah, he'll be here tomorrow. God, now he can shut up about seeing you again."

Now Quinn's leg is bouncing, so I take my turn and put my own hand on her thigh.

"Oh my god, what is happening?" Luca says and leaves quickly.

Ignoring him, I glance back to the couple and stand. I'm taller than this Sully guy by a good foot and about twice his size in muscle. Not that it matters, but I'm aware of the way he looks up at me and his eyes widen. "Hi, I'm Miles."

I offer my hand.

"Oh my god!" Andy squeals. "You're Miles."

Quinn is biting her bottom lip as she watches the interaction.

"Hey, man," Sully shakes my hand. "I'm Sullivan, but everyone just calls me Sully. This is my fiancée, Andy. It's so good to finally meet you."

What does he mean by *finally meet me*?

Hudson comes over to grab their drink order, so I take the chance to lean in Quinn. "Who are these people?"

"Friends," she says quickly.

"Yeah, and they are eager to meet me because …"

Her nose scrunches and she shakes her head.

"Tell me right now, Quinn."

She leans in even closer, her breath on my ear, but Andy speaks first, her voice thick with excitement.

"Anyway, so Danny and most of the group will be here tomorrow. This is kismet, Quinn. All of us being in the same place at the same time before the big day. I know I've said this already, but this summer is really going to be the best one."

Quinn's face turns pale as she looks up at me, those green eyes begging me to help her.

I don't show any reaction.

She's hiding something from me, and as much as I think it's going to be hard to pull this off and that pretending to date isn't the right path to go down, one thing is clear.

I'm going to be Quinn Bank's boyfriend for the next eight weeks.

CHAPTER SIX

QUINN

I'm a pretty put-together person. I like exactly two cups of coffee a day. I'd rather have a gummy daily vitamin than the hard ones that get lodged in my throat. I have to have matching pajamas sets at night. I like knowing that I don't need to rely on anyone else to make any choice in my life. It's my life.

Which is exactly why I hate that the moment Sully and Andy showed up, a sinking feeling hit my stomach. Like that first small instance when you think you're going to be sick. Your body sits up in a jerk and your brain thinks, *am I going to puke?*

I hate even more that Miles picked up on my odd behavior in the snap of someone's fingers. I was going to tell him about my slip-up last summer, but I thought maybe I could wow him with my office skills and show him how valuable I could be or maybe even get a little further with this Cherry thing to show him how it works, and then he wouldn't care that I had a plan, but now, I have to just rip off the Band-Aid.

That makes me nervous.

"Anyway, Andy's parents are sitting on the other side of the bar near the bookstore, but we wanted to come say hi," Sully says.

"We definitely need to do lunch or dinner, and oh gosh, you have to come to the wedding. Oh, and the festivals this town has. I hope we see you at all of them."

I'm about to tell them I'm going to be busy, but it makes me even more sick to lie more than I have.

Miles clears his throat next to me. I glance at him at the same time Andy and Sully do, and we all catch the way Miles's gaze falls to my hand on his thigh, his hand settled over mine.

"Oh my gosh, we are interrupting your lunch date. We will see you around." Andy smiles, leaning in to hug me one more time before they walk away.

We all wave goodbye just as our lunch appears.

I ignore the way I can feel Miles watching me.

I can practically feel the heat of his questions breathing on my neck. I roll my shoulders as if I can shake them off.

"Care to explain?" he says, slowly turning to eat his lunch.

"Not really."

He takes a bite of his burger, nodding.

Once he swallows, he says, "Let me rephrase that. Explain."

I roll my eyes and dip my French fry into the mustard on my plate. I make sure he's watching as I stick it in my mouth.

He cringes. "I want an explanation so much right now that I'll suffer through watching you eat that nasty shit. I'll watch you eat every single fry, Quinn."

"That bad, huh?"

"Well, I won't lie: you have the upper hand right now. I'm clearly in need of help in all areas of life and all of a sudden little Miss Perfect Quinn—oh, sorry, Quinny—shows up and saves the day. Yet, unexpectedly, it seems she might need some help of her own."

"Are you saying that you enjoy seeing me uncomfortable?"

He shakes his head.

"I like seeing that you're not as perfect as I thought you were."

I narrow my gaze at him.

What the hell kind of response is that? I'm opening my mouth to ask just that when he beats me to it.

"It's a compliment, Quinn. Up until this moment, you and I have had zero things in common. You feel a bit more human than you did an hour ago."

He might mean it as a compliment, but it doesn't feel that way.

"Just because we're different doesn't mean I'm less human. You do realize people are meant to be different. To be their own person. To mold their own path. Being different from someone else isn't wrong."

He blinks but then he just keeps staring at me.

"You're right. I'm sorry. But just so you know, if we are going to make this work, we need to be honest with each other."

He just goes back to eating his lunch, as do I, and we fall into a silence that I can't quite describe. It's not weird, but it's not good. It's like we both know that not talking is the right move right now.

Once we are finished and Hudson brings the bill, I try to grab it first.

"I'm paying," Miles says in a clipped tone.

"I can buy my own lunch."

"This was a work lunch, so it's on me."

"Just let me buy my lunch."

"I'll let you buy your lunch if you tell me what's going on."

I sigh and hop off the stool.

"Leave him a good tip," I say over my shoulder.

I walk out the door and instantly spot Cherry across the street. I don't think she sees me, but I feel defeated all the same.

Two months. I'm only here for two months. It shouldn't be that hard to do this.

Miles steps out of the bar, and Cherry's radar senses he's nearby. Before I can think better of it, I slide my hand into Miles's and start walking to the shop.

If we are going to make this work, he's right—he should know as much as he can.

"Andy and Sully got engaged last summer," I say as we walk. "Over the last few years, people I know have all been getting engaged or married, and when Sully proposed to Andy, that meant I was the only single one left in that group. I was tired of hearing them talk about how I needed to meet someone, so when they brought up my dating Danny, Sully's brother, I panicked and said I did have a boyfriend. I gave them your name."

"Jesus," he whispers. "Why?"

"Because the chances of them ever running into you seemed highly unlikely. I had no idea they'd come here for their wedding."

"Wedding and summer vacation," Miles adds. "So, you didn't come back to my shop yesterday because you wanted to help me."

"Not entirely. I knew I could help you and help myself at the same time."

Miles groans.

"This is going to turn into a mess."

"I know, but please don't change your mind. It's eight weeks. Once the summer is over and we go our separate ways, we can tell everyone we broke up and be done with it."

Miles doesn't say anything as we get closer to the shop.

"What else do you need to know?" I ask.

"What's the deal with this Danny guy?"

Now it's my turn to groan.

"One could say he's my very own Cherry."

"You hooked up with him?"

I slug Miles's shoulder.

"Shit, you can hit." He rubs his shoulder.

"It was two summers ago, and it was supposed to be a fling that was never going to last. I knew it, and I thought he did, too. It wasn't a secret that I was going to Madrid next to meet up with my parents and he was coming back to the States. I just thought we both knew what we were getting into. Turns out I was wrong. And I never slept with him. He was too … polite."

"Ah, so you like a good dick," he says and laughs. "Noted."

I move to slug him again, but he jumps back with his hands up.

"Okay, okay, not a joking moment, got it. So I'm guessing you didn't tell him to fuck off."

I do my best to contain my smile—Miles needs to learn how to joke—before I answer him.

"Nope."

"How did you end it?"

I take a deep breath at his questions.

"I may have assumed we'd never run into each other again. Heck, at that time, Andy and Sully were fighting, so there was a good chance I'd never see him again."

"What did you say?"

"I said something like if we were meant to be, then fate would find a way to put us back into the other's path."

Miles gags, and I laugh a little.

"That's awful."

"I was trying to let him down gently. I fully thought I'd never see him again."

"And now your friends think we've been dating for a year." He turns to glare at me. "And some guy who thinks you two are soulmates is here for the summer and …"

"A woman who thinks she should wait for you is also here for the summer and …"

"We are fake dating so that no one gets hurt and so your friends won't hound you to settle down," Miles finishes our conversation.

We stop outside Miles's shop, and he squeezes my hand twice. It happens so fast that I almost don't notice it.

But I do.

It reminds me of when my family, back before Mom, Dad, and I started traveling, would eat dinner together and hold hands, squeezing them three times for *I love you* before we began eating.

But twice?

It must have been some kind of muscle reflex.

"What does this say about our characters?" Miles asks.

"It says we both know what we want in life and what we don't want, so we're going to help each other out for the next eight weeks to make those things happen."

He turns and walks backward into the shop. "I guess it does."

Leaving the conversation at that, I make my way into the office and sit down.

I lied to make my life less complicated, and now that lie has complicated my life.

Talking to Miles is all fine and dandy, but I need someone who can talk this out with me who isn't invested the way I am.

I need Sadie.

———

As soon as the clock hit four, I left the office and went straight for B's Bakery. If I keep this to myself the entire summer, I'm going to lose my mind. I need someone who is familiar with this kind of thing.

The obvious answer is my brother. He writes romance novels with fake dating as a trope. But it's not for real life.

Which is exactly what he would tell me, and that's the reason I'm not going to him. I could go to Natalie, but she's Team Tobias all the way, so that's a no-go, too. Grandma Betty would read way too much into it, so I can't do that to her.

Sadie just makes sense because she owns a bookstore based on romance, possibly loves this trope and knows what we need to do, and of course, the obvious reason: she overheard enough yesterday that she knows something is up.

I clutch my purse tighter when I see the bakery's closed sign. Shit.

She hangs out here so much that I assumed she'd be here. I turn to my left and go to the bookstore attached to Hudson's Bar.

I don't see her when I walk in, so I start to browse the books. If I can't talk to her, getting a couple of books on fake dating seems like a smart move. Again, I could just borrow books from my brother, but no thanks. Reading the spicy books he writes is a big fat no for me.

I scan the shelves for the fake dating section. I grab the first book I find and start to read the back when a body down the row blocks the sunlight from the front window.

"Ah!" I say and drop the book.

"What are you doing?" Miles asks and then looks around like we are doing something illegal.

I squat to grab the book and start looking for another one.

"I'm doing research. What does it look like I'm doing?"

He marches over to me, takes the book from my hand, and shoves it back onto the shelf.

"Hey now, what did that book ever do to you?"

"Whatever you're doing here, it looks like you're about to give us away."

"By reading romance?"

"By being in this section. The big words *fake dating* are above you, and this town is just learning about our new relationship. If anyone were to see you, that's it. Deal done."

I look up at the sign, then turn to a different section. The single dad and nanny section shouldn't set off any alarms.

I sigh and grab a book, but now I'm not reading. I'm just trying to look busy.

"Why are you really here?" Miles asks, hovering around me.

"Why do you assume I'm here for something other than a book?"

"Because I saw how you snuck out of the shop, looking over your shoulder, all suspicious. You didn't want me to see you leave."

"Are you stalking me?" I shove the book into his chest before moving to another section.

"No, but I'm learning to read you fairly well, so spill."

He crosses his arms and steps into my space, waiting for me to speak. His gaze locks onto mine, flickering to my lips for the quickest moment.

I'm a little taken back at how much my body responds to his closeness. Well, how my nipples react anyway.

They like it.

Too much. So much that now I'm wondering why he looked at my lips. Did his body react the same way just now?

Like some weird electric current struck us both, since we were just inches apart.

Is he thinking of me in ways that the two of us should not be thinking of each other?

Did he think about kissing me? In the romance section no less. Now, *that* would secure our little secret.

I take a breath and then roll my eyes as to not give my real thoughts away. Thinking of Miles as anything more than my current accomplice would not be smart.

I'm about to tell him what Sadie overheard, then Sadie herself and Hudson step into view. They clearly don't see us, because before we know it, Hudson pins Sadie to one of the bookshelves and starts to kiss her.

Mile instantly clears his throat.

"This is a bookstore, not a live movie."

Hudson barely moves, as if the thought of taking his hands off Sadie is unbearable, as he turns to his brother.

Sadie is grinning, but her cheeks are rosy.

She looks wildly in love.

Those are the moments I want. Yeah, the moments my friends mentioned last summer were great, too, but the little moments like when he can't keep his hands off me or just looking at him makes me melt—that's what I want.

"Is there ever a part of your day where you two aren't touching or kissing? Jesus, it's getting to be a bit much," Miles adds.

I roll my eyes. Of all the things I want, this is what I get for the summer.

"Fancy seeing you two here," Sadie says. "I was actually going to go by your brother's later to talk to you, Quinn."

"Oh, yeah, um, I'm actually staying in the apartment behind the shop now."

"Oh, really? Miles, that's great that you stopped being a jerk long enough to do something nice for Quinn."

"It sounds like he's doing a lot more than being nice," Hudson says with a coy smile.

Sadie nods as if she doesn't need any more detail.

"Yes, well, it's about time."

"They're dating," Hudson adds.

"What?" Sadie snaps, but then she smiles. "Is this—" She rushes toward me and grabs my arm. "Come with me."

"No, no," Miles says quickly and grabs my hand. "Anything you have to say can be said in front of me, too."

"Oh, this is great," Hudson says, leaning onto a bookshelf.

Sadie looks from me to Miles to Hudson and back to me.

I toss up my hands.

"Sadie knows."

"What?" Miles snaps.

"She was at the bakery yesterday when Andy and Sully came in and asked about my boyfriend."

"To be fair, I'm the one who mentioned you first because you were being all sour, Miles, and not letting her stay in the apartment. Your name must have triggered something for them."

"Yeah, it triggered the fact that last summer, Quinn here told everyone that the two of us were dating," Miles says in a hushed tone. He barely has the words out before Hudson starts to crack up.

"It's not funny," Miles says quickly, but that doesn't stop Hudson. "I guess we can just call the whole thing off now."

"What? No?" I say quickly. "Why?"

"People know it's a lie." He holds his hand out to Hudson and Sadie.

"We won't tell anyone," Hudson says quickly. "Hell, if she takes things off your plate and all you have to do is hold her hand a few times and take her to a festival here or there, I'd say that's one hell of a deal."

"It's complicated, is what it is," Miles replies.

"It doesn't have to be," I cut in. "We can make this extra simple. If people ask, we say that we are dating, but we hate PDA, then we show up places to be seen and go back to our homes at the end of the night."

"Sounds easy enough," Sadie says.

She shares a glance with her fiancée, and he nods. No words, just a look, and even though it makes me suspicious, I love that unspoken bond thing, too.

"Fine, but let's go before we run into anyone else who just happens to know the truth." Miles grabs my hands and rushes us through the store to the front door.

"Aww, he's stealing you for alone time," Hudson calls out after us.

I can hear Sadie's laughter as the door shuts.

Miles's steps don't slow as we make our way back to the shop, which makes me laugh.

To any prying eyes, we look as Hudson just said.

Heck, we might be able to pull this off after all.

CHAPTER SEVEN

MILES

Someone slap me if I ever squeeze Quinn's hand like that again.

I did it as a reflex, but my mind—yeah, mind—said those two little words, and I bolted into the shop before she could sense I was about to start acting weird. I've never done that to anyone. Ever. The worry in her voice triggered it somehow. Like I felt her words more than heard them.

Was that what happened to my mom when she'd do it to me?

I obsessed over it the entire afternoon to the point that I finally decided to go say something to Quinn. But she wasn't in the office. I stepped out of the shop to see if she was outside, and that's when I saw her running off.

The glance over her shoulder was all I needed. She was about to do something I wouldn't approve of.

Finding her in that bookstore proved just that.

I scan my key card at the gym and wave at the kid working. I've seen him around, but his family must be new because I can't put a name to his face.

He nods and goes back to whatever he was doing.

I need this workout today something fierce because as if the whole deal with Quinn weren't enough, now my brother and Sadie know. I'm not even working out yet, and I'm already sweating over how this whole thing will play out. The boyfriend part, I mean. I don't date much, so if I were someone's boyfriend, I'd struggle at it, and now I'm a fake boyfriend.

What the hell do they even do?

I head straight for the locker room and spot Luca stuffing his bag into one of the lockers.

I set my gym bag down next to him.

"Hey," I say, and Luca slams his locker.

"No." He points in my face. "I'm mad at you."

"Why?" I pull out my pre-workout and change into my gym shoes.

Did Hudson tell him?

"Because at lunch yesterday, you drop this bomb on me that you're doing whatever with Quinn, and you have not called or texted me once to clarify. I'm at a loss here. Hanging on for dear life and waiting for answers."

It's a good thing he's not dramatic or anything.

"It sort of just happened," I tell him. Which, to be fair, is not a lie.

"I don't accept that as an answer," Luca says.

We leave the locker room and walk down the hallway that leads to the cardio section. We usually run a mile before we lift weights, and then we run another mile after. We started this routine in high school, and it stuck.

We claim two treadmills side by side and get going at a slight jog.

Do I tell him the truth? It would be weird for Hudson to know and not Luca, but Luca talks a lot. Too much sometimes, and this isn't something I want to accidentally slip.

"Who approached who?" he asks.

I turn up the speed. "She came to the shop and asked to rent out the apartment."

"And you just looked at her, fell in love, and said yes?"

I chuckle. "No. I told her to get lost."

As soon as the words are out of my mouth, I regret them. Those aren't the words of a man who suddenly fell for this girl.

"Sooo, then you felt bad and went to find her?" he asks. The confusion is clear as he says each word slowly.

"No. She returned, but this time she offered to help in the office. So then I said yes."

Technically, it's all true. Give or take a few details.

"Okay, and then you … spent the night together."

Okay, this needs to be the end of this conversation. Lying to my brother is wrong, so I need to choose my words carefully.

"Luca, I'll put it this way. You will be seeing a lot of Quinn this summer, and a lot of that time she will be with me. Things just happened with us, and this is where we are now. You'll have to accept it."

He nods. "Sure. I'll accept it … as soon as you beat me to a mile."

And then he sprints like he's never sprinted before.

I catch up quickly, and even though it burns and all I can focus on is not tripping or hitting the front of the treadmill with my foot and slipping, one thought occurs to me.

I'm pretty sure my brother knows I'm not telling him the truth.

Maybe it's a brother thing or maybe it's just twin intuition, but either way, he gives me weird looks throughout our entire workout. Or maybe it's because I hit a mile first by three seconds so he held back on asking more questions.

I follow him into the locker room, and as we both fill our water bottles and pour our protein power inside of them, he finally says, "Does she still plan on leaving at the end of the summer?"

"I think so, why?"

"Then why start anything with her?"

He holds my gaze for a moment, and that's when it hits me.

He's not snooping. He's worried.

My whole thing is to not date a tourist, but here I am, dating Quinn.

I shrug. "Sometimes … things just don't make sense." Which is true. "But what Quinn and I have going on right now, it feels right." Which is also true, despite the mental war I have over what to do and what not to do.

For now, this is our plan.

He nods, but I can see it on his face that he's not fully convinced.

We pack our bags and walk out the door.

We bump knuckles as a goodbye, then go our separate ways back to work.

I should tell him the truth and reassure him that he doesn't need to worry, but I don't.

Hell, if only he knew that Quinn leaving at the end of summer is the easiest part of this deal.

———

I SIT up and stretch my arms over my head, glancing at the clock on the wall behind me.

Shit.

It's almost ten at night.

I need to call it a day and get some sleep.

I stand up and stretch again. I've been in the same position for too long, but the issue I was having is fixed, so I can't really complain.

I wash my hands and then turn all the lights out and close the only shop door still open. Then I make my way out the back.

The office is all closed up, and the cleanest it's ever been.

A good boss would check on her work. I mean, hell, it's clean, but that doesn't mean anything.

I sit down at the computer, and as soon it comes to life, my email pops up. There are about twenty new replies unread.

The first one is a quick thank-you for sending the invoice. They want to know our banking information so they can transfer the payment.

Sweet.

The second one is the same, but they included check details of their payment in the mail today and are asking for my openings next year.

The next couple of emails are similar.

I lean back and let out a breath.

Fuck.

This is awesome.

I would have made time eventually because money does run out, so I'd need to get it somehow, but this is a relief. And I get this kind of help all summer.

I grin.

I'm going to sleep great tonight.

As I'm leaving, I spot something on the corner of the desk. It's a draft of an ad for help in the shop. Part-time mechanic. I scan it quickly; there is a question mark by the pay and the hours. She's written *how much* next to experience. She also wrote *ask him* next to job details.

I know she will ask me first thing, but I sit back down, grab a pen and answer her notes.

She's done so much for me already, it's my turn to do a little for her. Which is still helping me, but it's progress.

She'll get it.

I lock up and cross the small yard to my house. The porch light is on at the apartment and Quinn is rocking on the porch swing with a book. I spot her legs first, one crossed over the other.

Just once, I'd like to know if they are as soft as I imagine they are.

She looks up when I come fully into view, so I stop.

"Are you just now done working?" she asks, sitting up and setting her book down. She grabs her phone. "It's after ten."

I shrug. "I like my job."

She hums. Then she leans back again and grabs her book.

It's late and dark, but the end of spring air is warm, and tonight we are blessed without wind. It's the perfect night to hint that summer is almost here. Per the calendar, it'll be here in three days. Which also means Lovers will be having its annual first day of the summer festival.

One of many that happen during the year.

It's also an opportunity for Quinn and me to rip off the Band-Aid to the town and tourists.

"Do you need something?" she asks.

I nod, pointing to one of the chairs at the small table. "May I?"

She nods.

I take in her bare legs as she shifts. Of course I do. They're now tucked under her body to the side. She's wearing a matching short and top set, all white with yellow and pink flowers. The top covers everything and reminds me of a dress shirt the way it buttons up the front. Her hair is down, and her face is makeup-free.

It occurs to me that the Quinn online is very similar to the one right in front of me, and a little bit of guilt sets in. I assumed they were two different people, but it turns out, she doesn't pretend to be anyone else.

Shit. I don't know why I thought she did.

It actually reminds me of the first time I saw her.

It was the summer before my sophomore year of high school. She was in line at the ice cream shop with her grandma, Betty. Betty was talking to my dad, and Quinn was gazing through the glass at all the flavors. Not a care in the world about what was happening around her. When the woman working asked what she wanted, she said pistachio with cookie dough bites and crushed Reese's.

It didn't make any sense, but she didn't care. She wanted what she wanted, and that was that.

I remember thinking that I'd finally found another kid in Lovers who was as sure of themselves as I was.

Over an ice cream order.

Then I found out she wasn't here to stay. So I never tried to befriend her. What was the point? At that time in my life, I was tired of people leaving.

I formed my opinion of her that day and never let it go.

"Are you going to sit there in silence or tell me what's on your mind?"

I shake the memory away.

That was a long time ago.

"I think we should use the summer kickoff festival to make our relationship ... official."

"That's very public," she says quietly.

"Yeah, well, it beats having all these people ask me about us separately. This way, we can get it all out of the way and no more questions."

She smiles. "Are people asking you questions about us?"

"So far just Luca, but gossip spreads fast in a small town. I have no doubts that our lunch yesterday will have raised questions."

She nods.

"Maybe. No one in my family asked me about it."

"Have you seen them since we had lunch?"

"No, but I've texted with my grandmother and I've dropped coffee off for my brother and his wife. Not one word about me hanging out with you."

I sigh. "Fine, so this will be for me."

"Okay," she says as if it's that easy.

I stand quickly and plop myself right next to her. She leans away from me.

"That. Right there. You can't do that when we are together," I tell her. "Not in public anyway."

She scoffs. "I know I can't. You didn't see me pulling away at the bar, did you?"

"No."

She's right. She didn't. In fact, it sort of felt natural with her.

"You need to stop overthinking this. I get the vibe that you've been obsessing over this plan of ours since we agreed to it. Which reminds me, thank you. I know you were seconds away from calling the whole thing off before … well, you were there."

I nod.

"I am obsessing. It's just weird. This was not how I imagined my summer."

"Nor did I, but it's going to be fine. It's not forever, and the time is going to pass quickly. It always does."

Her voice softens at her last few words, which makes me think she has a double meaning, but right now, her feelings are not my concern. My concern is how we pull this off without anyone ever finding out that we lied.

And in my mind, there is only one way to do this.

"Okay. We don't go anywhere in town without the other," I say. "If your family needs you, I'm there. If my family needs me, you're there. We attend every single event together. We make plans with other couples together. We eat together. Whatever it is, we do it together."

"That seems excessive. What if I want to go have coffee or lunch with the girls?"

"Are you here often enough to have people you can call 'the girls'?"

"Yes." She swats my arm. "Believe it or not, most of the people in this town have accepted me."

"Most, not all."

"Well, technically, now they all have. The last one decided he would just date me instead."

Her eyebrows dance.

I just stare at her.

"Sadie, Brooke, and Natalie are who I consider the girls, if you wanted to know. If you don't let me go anywhere without you, they will be suspicious."

"Brooke and Natalie might, but Sadie will get it for obvious reasons," I say as I stand.

"What does that mean?"

I take a couple of steps off the porch toward my house before I turn around.

"Because, even if she didn't know this was fake, the Asher men love nothing more than to spend time with the ones they care about. That now includes you, Quinn."

The smile she gives me is a soft one.

"We really should make more rules than what you just told me."

I cross my arms and grin. "I told you mine. You tell me yours."

She stands up and comes down the steps until she's practically toe to toe with me.

"We hold hands, we always sit by each other, and you kiss me on the cheek or the forehead. No lips."

"Cheeks and forehead?"

She nods. "It's a gesture that shows how much you care without showing too much affection in public. Women love forehead kisses. It'll work. Trust me."

I nod. "Okay. Deal."

Quinn reaches her hand out for me to shake.

I slip my hand in hers, and she says, "Deal."

We have a plan, we have rules, and we seem to be getting along a lot easier than I expected.

Looks like we might be able to pull this off after all.

CHAPTER EIGHT

QUINN

Turns out fake dating is easy when you don't go out in public.

Miles and I made a plan, but since that plan wasn't set to start until the weekend, we basically kept a low profile around town. This might turn out to be a lot easier than I thought. We just work and go home. Separately. All of it separately, unless you count the couple of encounters when I'm sitting on the porch and he's going home much later than the average person should be working.

There have been a few applicants for the shop position, but I haven't interviewed them yet. I want Miles to be there, so I'm still working on a time when I can do them all in an hour of his day and be done with it.

He's busy, and I'm here to make his life easier.

However, tonight is the summer kickoff festival, and it's a big night for us.

I run my fingers through my hair and fluff it a little for volume. I curled it, which isn't something I do often, because I have so much hair that it takes me at least a half hour. Which almost defeats the fluffing purpose, but I'll take what I can get.

Some girls would kill for hair like mine, but it's so heavy that it'll be flat in twenty minutes, and don't even get me started on pulling it back. I have no doubt that girls with thick hair are stocked up on painkillers.

I grab my dark pink lip gloss and glide it on just as there is a knock at the back door.

I step out of the bathroom and wave Miles in.

"I just need another minute," I tell him.

He nods, walking into the living room.

I finish my lips, spray myself with perfume, then slip on some strappy wedges.

"What the hell is that?" Miles points at me.

I glance down at my shirt and then at my jeans and shoes. What?"

"Your shirt."

I smile. "You don't like it?"

"I think it's overkill."

"No, it's not, " I say and hold my hands out so he can read the entire thing. "We're going for a vibe that says we fell hard and we fell fast," I say. "It's perfect."

"No. Can you change?"

"I cannot." I laugh. "It's fine."

He groans, running a hand through his hair. "I cannot go to this event with you wearing a shirt that says Dibs on the Mechanic in bold letters."

"You can and you will. Who cares what people think anyway? This isn't real. We are just playing a part to avoid breaking hearts. Let's go."

"You know," he says as he follows me out the door, "I'm not really looking forward to this."

"Yes, I can sense that."

"The part where we will be the focus of attention, I mean.

I'm not used to it. Plus, I think I should tell Luca. It feels weird that Hudson knows and not him."

I pause.

When I first started posting online, not many people liked, commented, or even followed me. As all of that increased, I was uneasy at first, but then it got easier because I wasn't doing anything but being myself. As long as I stayed true to that, it didn't matter to me who was paying attention and who wasn't.

"First off, if you want to tell Luca, I trust your judgment. Second, outside of the fact that we are going together, nothing has to change. You can still sit with your family like you always do, you can drink beers if that's what you want. Snack on some appetizers. You can sit in the same spot the entire time and let people come to you. Nothing has to be different other than your company."

He nods.

"But you do need to act like you like me. That might help."

I turn to walk away, and he's hot on my heels.

"I know that," he scolds as we head toward Main Street and the festival. "That part isn't a problem."

"Good, now take a breath. You plan to work all summer, and I plan to do whatever I want. We don't have to make a ton of appearances if we don't want to. I mean, we could play this off as we are goal-driven people who like to stay in. Easy."

"It doesn't feel like it's going to be easy."

"That's because you're still obsessing over how it won't work."

"It might not, and we—"

"Quinn!" Brooke shouts and waves me over to where she, Sadie, Hudson, Luca, and Sadie's brother are sitting under a tent right between Hudson's bar and B's Bakery.

"We saved you both a spot," Sadie says as we sit down.

"Yeah, both of you," Luca says with a smile.

"Thank you," I say honestly and face Miles's twin. They're fraternal, so it's not like I'm looking at Miles's duplicate, but Luca also has sharp features, and they both have the same bright blue eyes and dark scuff.

When Miles sits, he leaves enough room between us for another full-grown adult to take, so I casually scoot next to him. "Do you want to go get us something to drink?"

"Yeah," he says quickly.

Luca, Linc, and Hudson stand, too.

"We all need refills," Hudson says.

Miles glances over his right shoulder to look at me as they all walk toward the bar. He glances at Luca quickly, and I take that as he's going to tell him.

I nod to reassure him that's fine.

"Oh god, look at him. He's smitten."

Smitten? More like he's a wreck.

"He's a little nervous about tonight," I admit.

"Why would he be nervous?" Sadie asks, clearly playing her part.

"Because this thing between us is so new and sudden, and he's … I don't know. I'm nervous, too."

"Makes sense," Brooke says. "I don't think I've ever seen him date. Not in a way that he'd make such a public appearance like this one." She nods at something behind me. That's when I notice there are a lot more people in town looking in our direction.

Specifically, Cherry's father.

I did some social media research that first night in Miles's apartment. It was more for Cherry, but her dad was everywhere on her account. Apparently, this guy is a big deal. Some of the things I read were pretty intimidating. He's the kind of man who gets what he wants and could make or break someone's career.

Truth be told, that kind of power in life sounds too stressful for me.

Our eyes meet, and he nods. Clearly, he knows who I am.

I smile and wave.

I turn to go back to the conversation with the girls, but instantly the hairs on my neck come to attention.

"Hey, Quinn," a voice says right behind me, and I don't need to turn around to know who it is.

Danny.

I turn slowly and grin.

"Hey," I say casually.

His hands are stuffed in his pockets. "How have you been?"

"Good. How about you?"

"Good. I was excited to hear that you were also going to be here this summer."

"Yeah, Lovers is amazing."

I quickly glance at the girls, who all look away as if they aren't watching us.

"I heard that you were still seeing someone," he says.

"I am."

"Is he here?"

I'm opening my mouth to answer, but someone beats me to it.

"Yes, he is."

Danny spins and steps back, revealing Miles and his brothers.

The look in Miles's eyes is dark. He sets our drinks down and sits at the table, one leg on each side of the bench, with me sitting between them.

And then he kisses my temple. It wasn't the cheek or the forehead, but I'll accept it.

And it seems to be the gesture that makes everyone accept our relationship as well.

"I'm Miles," he finally says to Danny.

"Danny."

They shake hands.

"I hope you guys enjoy Lovers over the summer. It's the best time of the year to be here. The lake is warm, and the mountain has trails to explore for days."

"Yeah," Danny says hesitantly. "I'm looking forward to it. I think I might be most interested in the festivals I've heard you all have here. I'm a big-city guy, so this will be good for me. A refreshing break."

"That's what we're here for. A wonderful palate-cleansing town."

Danny smiles, but I don't miss the tone of Miles's last comment.

He's insulted.

This is his town.

His family.

His friends.

And Danny just let him know it's only good for a break.

Something I've said before, too. Never out loud, though. But it makes a lot of things about Miles clearer to me.

"Well, see you around," I say to Danny, and he nods, waving at the table as he leaves.

Everyone is quiet for a moment, eyes on me and Miles.

Miles leans in and whispers, "Did you really just tell him you'd *see him around*?"

The humor is back in his voice, and I can't help but smile wider.

I turn to him, my nose brushing his unintentionally.

"Maybe."

His eyes lock on mine, and he shakes his head.

"Now you're just asking for me to tease you."

"Okay stop, stop," Luca says rather loudly, causing me to jump back.

I forgot they were here.

"I can't have you two making out"—he points at Hudson and Sadie, then to me and Miles—"and have you two be all swoony over each other all summer long."

Miles enjoys a deep belly laugh that instantly warms my heart.

"You better get used to it." He wraps his arms around my shoulders, pulling me close.

Wow, he's oddly good at this.

"I sure hope there's room at this table for two more," Grandma Betty and Mike join us. Her gaze flickers to Miles's arm, then to my eyes. She smiles, but she doesn't say a word.

"There is always room for you, Betty," Sadie says.

Conversation quickly falls into the summer activities. In a few weeks, there will be the July 4th Blast, followed by the Lovers 4th of July, which is something only the locals know about. Then there is the end-of-summer party the first week of August before the kids go back to school. The town has decided to make that the biggest one of the season.

"So not only will the contest take place, but the bar and bookstore will have a spot. The dance studio is right next to us, so you can dance, then grab a drink and a snack, then a book, all in one smooth move."

"Now, we all know I love to read. It's not a secret in our family that we love books, but I'm not sure that'll be the first thing on my mind to do when I'm at a town party," Grandma Betty says.

"Probably not, but since tourists can come and I have exclusive signed editions from some very well-known authors"—Sadie winks at my grandmother—"that will change minds pretty quickly."

Grandma laughs. "That reminds me. Natalie asked to place an order for some of those blueberry muffins in the morning. I need to go find Brooke."

She begins to stand, but Mike puts his hand on her arm. "Let me go do it, dear. I'll be right back."

Grandma smiles at him and then sits back down.

"Speaking of Natalie, are she and Tobias going to make it tonight?" I ask.

"Not tonight. They are exhausted but finally beginning to set some kind of sleep schedule. If those babies go to sleep early tonight, Mom and Dad will be, too."

"Makes sense," I say.

Miles is talking with Hudson and Luca, but he soon shifts his attention to me.

He smiles, which makes me do the same.

"So, how did this happen?" Grandma Betty asks.

"Yes." Luca rubs his hands together as he watches us.

Miles lets out a laugh as he leans around me to address Grandma Betty.

"Trust me, we are just as shocked as everyone else. But sometimes, things just … work out. Plus, she was pretty relentless when it came to my apartment. I mean, talk about being obsessed with me."

I let out a laugh and playfully swat his thigh.

He's not completely wrong.

"Well, I don't care how it happened. I'm just glad it did." Grandma pulls me in for a hug and then smacks the table. "You officially have a date for my wedding. Now, I'm going to go see what's taking Mike so long then probably call it a night." She kisses the top of my head. "You two come over for dinner soon, all right? Summers with Quinn are my favorite because I don't get to see her much."

I give her a quick hug and watch her go toward the bakery.

Mike walks out, reaches for her hand, and kisses the back of it. He never lets go as they walk down the street toward their house.

When my grandpa passed away, I wasn't sure how my grandma would get past that. How do you move on from losing the love of your life? How do you go through that kind of pain and come back from it?

Day by day, I guess. And now she's in love again.

The guys next to me let out a loud laugh.

Yeah, Grandma's been in love twice now, and I'm over here faking it.

———

"I'M GOING to put the two of you down as contestants for the bake-off at the Fourth of July festival," Brooke says as she brings out a plate of treats.

She's been sneaking different dishes out to tables all night to see what's the most popular. She says it's helpful when she actually has a booth set up. She'll know what to make more of.

"I'm not sure that's something we want to do," I say and look at Miles to back me up. Partaking means more appearances, and we know how he feels about that.

"What? Why not?" Brooke asks as she sits down. "You bake and drink beer. It's not a hardship."

Miles smirks at me, but truth be told, I think he wants to get as far away from me as possible.

Why?

Oh, because I told him this would be easy about three hours ago, and by this point in the night we have been invited on a hike with his brother and Sadie, his dad texted him to say he's sorry he missed us tonight but bring me by the house, Grandma Betty invited us over for dinner and said to bring him to her wedding as my date, Tobias messaged me that they want us over for beers, and now Brooke wants us to join the next festival for the bake-off they have every summer.

So my plan that we can lay low isn't working out very well.

"She's right," Miles says and leans back. "It's not a half bad deal."

"Can you even bake?" I ask, looking in his direction.

His eyes widen for a split second before they relax, and he smiles.

Shit.

That came out with much more snark than your typical girl-friend should have in her voice.

"I can bake. I just don't because B's is the best."

He's not wrong. Unless I'm in France, I've yet to find a bakery as savory as hers.

"All right, count us in," I say and grin.

"Perfect."

"We should be going," Miles says and stands abruptly.

I follow suit, agreeing that we need to get out of here before anyone else asks us to commit to something.

No isn't really in my vocabulary.

I give Brooke a hug, and Miles does the same before we start our walk back to the shop.

"Did you tell Luca?" I ask.

"Not yet. I was going to, but I figured I needed a less public place to do it. He's going to have a lot to say."

"Good point."

We make it about five steps before Andy, Sully, Ashley, and Danny spot us.

"Quinn, Miles, just the two people we were looking for," Andy says. "Danny mentioned you said there were trails around here. Would you two be up for showing us around some this weekend?"

"Oh, we have plans," Miles says quickly.

I nod in agreement.

"Oh, what are you doing? Is there another festival?"

I purse my lips and look up at Miles.

Say something.

Anything.

Come on, Miles.

"I'm getting a dog," are the words that come out, and I'm not sure who is more stunned by that unexpected response, me or the group in front of us.

"A dog," Sully says.

"Yep. We're getting a puppy," I add, as if that's going to help.

"A dog. Together?" Danny repeats, as if we all need it to be clarified.

"Yes" is all I have to say.

"You two must be serious then."

I nod and so does Miles, but neither of us actually say a word.

"A pet is a commitment. I think that's really good for you, Quinn," Danny adds.

The backhanded comment reminds me of what he said when I told him that we could only be just friends.

You won't be happy alone forever. You'll regret this.

Thankfully, the loud huff Miles makes next to me cuts that memory short. "What's that supposed to mean?"

Danny stands taller and steps back.

"Nothing. I just … she … I think it's great that she's committing to something other than her—"

"Finish that sentence." Miles crosses his arms and steps forward. "I dare you."

Danny holds his hands up in surrender.

"I didn't mean to be rude. I'm just stating a fact."

Miles then backs up and puts one hand at the base of my spine.

"If the fact you're trying to make is that Quinn is a confident and independent woman who should sure as hell always chooses herself over everyone in this world, than yeah, you're right. If you were going to say anything else, I'd choose your words carefully."

Danny keeps his mouth shut and nods.

"Well, if you feel like taking the new pup out on an adventure, you have my number and you know where to find us," Andy says, changing the subject quickly. "Have a good night."

"Night," I say, finally finding my words.

Miles doesn't reply. Instead, the hand at my lower back nudges me to keep walking.

Since we aren't exactly friends, I expect him to remain silent until we part ways at the shop, but he does the exact opposite.

I'm not even sure those four are out of earshot before Miles starts asking questions.

"Do they always talk to you like that?"

I shake my head.

"Really? Because you didn't seem surprised by his comment back there, and now that I think of it, if you felt you needed to lie about your dating life for whatever reason, maybe they aren't good friends to have."

"No, I guess I'm not surprised. I really only travel with them. They don't know much about me, which was why I was able to lie so easily."

"So, they do talk to you that way."

"Not all of them."

"Jesus, Quinn, I might have my opinions when it comes to you, but I'd never think for one second that I know what's better for you. What a fucking prick."

I grin at that.

"I can't believe you stood up for me back there." I shove his arm. He trips off the sidewalk and then steps back on. "Thank you."

"Well, there's only room for one guy in this town to be a dick to you, and I call dibs."

I roll my eyes, and that makes him laugh.

"But seriously, Quinn. Why do you hang out with people who talk to you that way?"

I hold a finger up.

"Technically, I hang out with Andy. She's sweet. She just so happens to hang around people I don't care for. And you've done your fair share of unkindness toward me."

He nods as if he gets it.

"I can admit when I've been wrong, but I also think you left out a few key pieces of your split with Danny from me."

I sigh. "It wasn't much, and I didn't think it mattered. He said I'd regret not taking a chance on him and I wouldn't figure it out until I was alone on a beach somewhere and it would be too late."

"So basically, he's an insecure jackass who doesn't deserve you anyway."

"Something like that." I don't look up at him because I know those last three words didn't hold as much positivity as the others.

What Danny said to me was wrong, yes, but it doesn't mean he was completely wrong. I do pick myself over everything else. It's how I got to where I am today. It's how I built my career and my image.

And that doesn't make it wrong.

I just … I don't know.

Something feels off with me. It helps that I'm working in the office. I like being needed.

No one ever usually needs me for anything.

We reach the shop and both head in the direction of the apartment.

"Well, get some rest, Quinn. It looks like we have an eventful summer on our hands."

I wrinkle my nose as I make a yikes smile. "Yeah, I wasn't expecting to be invited to that many places. I truly did think people would hear we are together, and the rumor mill would do the rest so we wouldn't have to make a show of it."

I unlock the sliding door.

Miles is right behind me.

"Well, you see, that's the thing about small towns. Your business is everyone's business, and lucky for you, my family is well known around here."

"Yes, lucky for me."

He grins and then backs up, pointing a finger at me.

"Just remember, this was all your idea."

"I didn't see you trying very hard to change my mind," I call out as he heads for his house.

He lifts a hand into the air to let me know he heard me, but he doesn't reply.

That's okay. He doesn't need to. Sticking up for me told me everything I needed to know.

Miles Asher is a good guy, and the two of us might actually be friends.

CHAPTER NINE

MILES

A seven-week-old golden retriever stares back at me from the brightness of my screen.

After I got home last night, if I wasn't thinking about Quinn, I was thinking about the dog I said I was going to get.

I've always wanted a dog but never pulled the trigger to get one. I'm a busy guy. I wouldn't have a ton of time to take care of one, but honestly, it'll never happen unless I make the time.

I click out of the site and check my emails.

Yep, you guessed it. I sent an inquiry for one of the pups. I figured if I was lucky enough to find some for sale in Wind Valley, just a couple hours away, then I better reach out.

I set my phone down and crawl out of bed.

It's early, but not as early as a typical workday. Even though I'll work in the shop later, I let myself sleep in an extra hour, sometimes two, on Sundays.

Then I go to breakfast at my dad's house.

Fuck.

I scrub a hand over my face.

The whole idea that this deal with Quinn would be easy was shot right out of the window in one night. I have no clue how I thought we could pull this off low-key.

Nothing about this town is low-key.

Once people start talking, everyone knows everything.

I shower and get ready quickly, pulling on some gray sweatpants and a black T-shirt. I slip on shoes and then lock the door as I head over to get Quinn.

She doesn't know that I'm coming.

She knows about breakfast, but we never established a time.

I never got around to it once we ran into her friends.

Friends. Ha. If you could call them that.

Friends wouldn't have let Danny talk to her like that.

Friends would have defended her.

No one did that for her.

And what a sad asshole for thinking she should pick him over herself. If I had to pick and he was my option, I wouldn't have picked him either.

I knock on the sliding door, stepping back so that I'm not right in her face when she opens it.

It's just after eight. I hope she's awake.

It takes her a moment, but she pulls the curtain back and smiles.

It's simple. A smile. A freaking smile. But something about it gets to me.

Not to mention the fact that she looks ready in every way but her clothes.

"Good morning, Miles," she says as soon as the door slides open. She crosses her arms and leans on the doorway.

She's wearing another set of those matching pajama ensembles with shorts and a shirt that buttons down the front. I do my best not to let my gaze wander down to her bare legs, but it's hard.

She's got really fucking nice legs.

She has nice everything: legs, ass, chest, smile, if I'm being honest. But until recent events, I never let myself look for too long.

I shouldn't be letting myself look now, but the more time we spend together, the harder it is not to.

Quinn is beautiful.

"What can I do for you?" she asks.

I snap my gaze to hers and then scratch the back of my neck.

"We have breakfast at my dad's this morning."

"Yeah, I was wondering what time that would be."

"I forgot to tell you that part last night, but then I realized that I don't have your phone number. Otherwise, I would have texted you when I did remember so that I wasn't springing it on you this early."

"Okay, how fast do I need to finish getting ready?"

"Twenty minutes?"

She nods. "Come in. I can be faster than that."

She turns and heads for the bedroom, and my sight falls straight to her ass.

Of course it fucking does, and her shorts are so short in the back that just a sliver of her cheeks show.

Fuck.

I take a breath and scrub a hand over my face.

Being attracted to Quinn isn't new for me, but being attracted to her and being around her this much without arguing is.

"Is this a special occasion?" she asks as she moves from the bedroom to the bathroom across the hall.

"No. Just Sunday breakfast."

With some kind of makeup wand thing in her hand, she pokes her head out to look at me.

"You do this every Sunday?"

"Yep."

"You, your brothers, and your dad."

"Yep. And now Sadie. Then Ruby and Max when they're in town."

"I've never met Ruby," she says loudly from the bathroom.

Because I'm used to looking at someone when they are talking to me, I turn to face where her voice is coming from and catch the exact moment she tosses her pajamas across the hall and back into the bedroom.

I would have taken her for the type of woman who takes her clothes off and folds them neatly to keep things tidy for when she needs to change back into them tonight.

"How often does she come to town?" Quinn asks, reminding me that we are talking about my little sister and not about what Quinn does with her clothes when she takes them off.

"Not as often as we all wish she would."

Quinn walks out of the bathroom, ready to go with a smile.

"Is this okay?"

She's wearing white cotton shorts and a green tank top with thick straps.

I nod. "It's perfect."

I open the door for her and lead her in the opposite direction of Main Street. Of all the Ashers, Dad lives the farthest from main street, and even then, it's still within walking distance for each of us.

"I've never been to your dad's house," Quinn says.

"That's pretty obvious."

"I mean, I don't think I even know where he lives."

"What? But aren't you basically a small-town local?" I tease, and she shoves me.

"Okay, I think you've made your point on that one. I was wrong. Just because I visit here as much as I do doesn't make me a local."

"Ah, she's learning."

"I am."

Her admission makes me smile, and I don't really know why.

Is it because she's agreeing with me, or is it because the conversation between us flows easily when we aren't fighting?

The screen door swings open as we reach the sidewalk in front of my father's house.

"I was hoping you'd bring Quinn," Sadie says.

"She's here," I say and follow both women inside.

Dad hugs me, and then he does the same to Quinn.

"Quinn Banks, it's so good to see you again. Of all the places in Lovers, my kitchen on a Sunday morning wasn't what I expected, but I am already a fan."

"Thank you, Mr. Asher. I love that you all do this."

"It is pretty cool, but I'm sure waking up to have a pastry in Europe or someplace exotic is more exciting."

"To be fair," Quinn says as we all move into the dining room where Luca and Hudson are sitting, "I think a family breakfast is more exotic than anything else in my life."

She takes a seat next to Sadie, so I take the other. Bacon, eggs, toast, pancakes, a quiche Sadie made, and a couple of muffins from B's are laid out in front of us. It seems like a bit much, but we all divide the leftovers and take them home to get us through most of the week.

Everyone dives in, dishing up their plates. My dad asks, "Does your family not do something similar?"

Quinn shakes her head as Luca passes her the quiche. "If you think I travel a lot, you should meet my parents. They taught me everything I know, and you already know Tobias is doing his own thing. I just … I don't see my family as much as I should."

Dad nods. I know he's about to say more on the subject, but I also caught the way Quinn's last sentence caught a little in her throat.

It makes me think of last night again, and for a reason I can't explain, I get pissed off all over again.

If she doesn't see her family often and her so-called friends clearly suck, who does she spend time with?

"So, Hudson," I cut in before my dad can drill Quinn on anything more that might become too personal. "Are you actually going to work at the bar's booth this year at the 4th of July festival?"

My older brother scowls at me, but he nods.

"Good. Wouldn't want you to skip out again this year."

"I didn't skip out last year," Hudson says, growing defensive. "I was busy."

"For good reason," Sadie adds quickly. She reaches for his hand on the top of the table, and the ring on her left hand shimmers in the light.

"Have you two picked a date yet?" Quinn asks.

"Next summer." Sadie beams.

"We thought we'd keep the day she showed up at my door as a tradition. Last summer, she showed up begging me to take her in," Hudson starts to tease, and Sadie pinches his side. He laughs and then kisses her forehead. "This year, I proposed on that same date, and next year, we will get married."

"I love that." Quinn sighs. "It's very romantic."

It is. Which, until last summer, was very unlike my brother, but again, as I said, I'm happy for him.

"How's the marina thing going?" I ask, turning my attention to Luca.

"It's not going. Shay hired someone from out of state, and it's complete bullshit. She wouldn't even give me five minutes. Told me I wasn't worth it."

No one says anything right away because this is a sensitive topic for Luca. Lovers is all about supporting each other, so for Shay to not hire him feels personal.

Which, to be fair, is for this particular situation.

"Who is Shay?" Quinn asks before I can stop her.

Hudson and Sadie groan, my dad shakes his head, and I open my mouth to give the shortest short version, but Luca is faster.

"Shay is my ex-best friend's sister. Her family owns the marina and apparently still despises me for something that happened thirteen years ago, because when one of Lovers's most popular attractions needed updating, they chose to hire anyone but the local contractor. That contractor is me," he added.

As if Quinn couldn't piece that together for herself.

I pinch my lips together to keep from laughing.

The situation as a whole is not funny, but damn, Luca's delivery sure is.

"What did you do to make their family hate you so much?"

"That's a damn good question, Quinn," I say and look at Luca.

Since none of us know the answer, the rest of the table joins me in watching my brother until he gives us the answer.

Which, of course, he doesn't.

"I'll be fine. Time heals all wounds."

I chuckle at that one and continue eating.

Conversation flows easy from there and it's mostly wedding talk, which gives me time to let my mind take a break. With Quinn here, it's like I need to be on high alert, ready to field any questions or slip-ups that could result in digging the hole we have created bigger than it currently is.

But shit, there's no backing out now. We've come too far.

And I want to tell Luca, but then I'll need to tell my dad, and I can see in his eyes that he's happy about me dating someone. I just—fuck, I don't know what I'm doing.

"So, we should go sometime this week," Sadie says, pulling me back into the conversation.

"Do what?"

"Go hiking," Quinn says and pats my leg as if she knows I'm about ten seconds away from losing it if we add more to our list of fake appearances. To be fair, this one had been mentioned already. We just didn't set a time. At least with them, it'll be a true hike and no need to fake anything about it.

My gaze drops to where Quinn touches me. Women have touched me before, and I'm an adult male who can handle it, but the fact that she hasn't removed her hand is what gets me. Or rather, it's that a small side of me doesn't want her to.

It's a hand on my thigh, for fuck's sake, and yet the action soothes me.

I look up to find Lucas glaring at me.

"This week is great," Quinn says, "but we should get going. I have a long list of shop candidates to look through, and we all know this man right here doesn't ever take a day off."

"But he should start," my dad chimes in, giving Quinn a goodbye hug. "Maybe having someone like you start stealing his time will knock some sense into him."

"Loving your job isn't a crime, Dad," I tell him.

"No, no, it's not, but missing out on life when it's happening right in front of you is."

I hold his gaze for a moment.

Before my mom died, Dad worked a lot. It wasn't until after she passed away so quickly that he started talking like this. *Live life to your fullest, Miles. Enjoy it while you can, Luca. Love like this only comes around once in your lifetime, Hudson.* There are so many more one-liners he recites to us, but the one he just said to me is right on par with the rest.

I know he didn't regret anything when it came to his relationship with Mom, though. Oh hell, those two are going to be one tough combination to beat.

I should know. I've been looking for a love like that for the last few years. Hence, why I made such a poor decision last summer with Cherry.

Which is also exactly why I'm not mad that Quinn blurted to her friends that she's dating someone. Just because others around you are falling in love doesn't mean you should force it when it's not your turn, but that doesn't stop us from wanting to feel something similar. Even for a brief moment.

I get it.

"I'll make sure he's having plenty of fun," Quinn says. She rests a hand on my back, rubbing it gently before she heads for the door. "See you next Sunday if not before then."

"I like her," my dad says before I can leave. "She's different."

I huff a laugh. "Oh yeah, she is."

"It must be why you picked her."

He slaps a hand on my shoulder before turning back for the kitchen.

As soon as I catch up to Quinn, my hand gravitates to her lower back as if it were an action I do every single day. I drop it as soon as I notice, but then we turn the first corner, and I do it again.

She turns to look at me, a small smirk on her lips right before she bites that damn bottom lip.

"Thanks for coming," I say quickly before I can think about her mouth any more than a man should.

"Of course. That was really nice."

"You know, I was thinking that if we can pull off moments like the one we just had with my family all summer long, we very well just might be the best fake dating couple this world has ever seen."

Quinn laughs.

She might think I'm cracking a joke, but I'm being serious.

Everything about today felt natural. I was ready for a day of playing this role, but the only person I had to be was me.

There is a very good chance that we get away with this.

If anything, it'll be the summer I finally get to know Quinn Banks.

CHAPTER TEN

QUINN

I didn't sleep very well last night, so as soon as I heard Miles unlocking the shop door, I stepped out and followed him, ready to go to work.

Although, to be fair, I hustled last week, and now that everything is organized, I maybe have an hour's worth of work to check emails and walk to the post office. Most people pay online now if that's an option, but maybe someone will pay by check and then I can add going to the bank to my list of tasks for the day.

I'm sure my days seem mundane and boring, but for me, the fact that I know I'm helping Miles, even if it's small, makes me feel good.

I type the password into the computer and wait for new emails to load.

Traveling is great, don't get me wrong. I love everything about visiting new places, but I think I've given off this vibe that I'm not available to those who need me. Like, maybe I've given the impression that all I know how to do is get on a plane or smile for a photo.

I mean, my grandma is getting married, and when I asked her if she wanted me to come back to help her plan, she said no, just take care of myself.

When Tobias told me the twins' due date, I told him I'd come back early, and he said no, don't rearrange your schedule for us.

My parents were going to Vienna for a couple of weeks, and I asked if they wanted company since we hadn't seen each other in a few months, but they said they had their days full and would meet up with me soon.

Either no one really needs me or they think that because I love to travel, that's all I am. As if traveling is my only personality.

Not a loving daughter, aunt, or granddaughter. Not Quinn Banks, a woman who would drop everything if her family asked her.

I'm a lot more than some girl who travels, and the only person who seems to have noticed that recently is Miles Asher.

I let out a little laugh.

That's one of the craziest thoughts I've ever had.

There are a couple of notifications for payments made, which impresses the heck out of me at how fast they came in, so I transfer the total to the checking account. Then, I print a couple of job applications we received over the weekend.

A yawn takes over, which makes sense. It's early.

I could make coffee, but a walk to get something better will help wake me up before I review these new applicants for the shop position.

I grab my purse and step into the garage.

Miles has all three bay doors open, and the sunrise that peeks in makes me pause.

Is this why he comes to work so early? If I were promised this view every morning, I'd wake up for it.

I snap a quick photo. It's not for my social account. It's for me. I want to remember this view after I leave at the end of the summer.

"Hey, you're up early," Miles says, stepping around his current project. It's blue with a horse on the front of the grill. He'd know the exact name, but I don't know anything other than Mustang.

"Yeah, I couldn't sleep," I tell him, sparing him the details as to why. "I thought I'd get a jump start to the day, but I need coffee and probably a donut because it's Monday, and that's reason enough."

"Are you walking to B's?"

I nod.

"I'll come with you."

I roll my eyes. "I don't think the town will be on high alert to see our relationship this early in the morning, so I can manage alone."

"You're probably right, but I'm not coming for that reason. I'm coming because I want something, too."

"I can just grab it for you."

He pauses and tilts his head. "If I recall, you told me that this deal of ours doesn't need to change our daily routine. Mine includes occasionally walking to B's for coffee. So, let's go."

He marches past me, and my eyes drift to his backside. Specifically, to where his jeans hug his ass.

Miles knows how to wear jeans better than any man I've met. I also love that he's a simple T-shirt guy. His tattoos are accessory enough. And I really like the backward hat look today.

All in all, Miles looks good, and for some reason, that makes my heart race a little more than normal.

I quickly catch up before he can spot me checking him out.

"Why couldn't you sleep last night?" he asks to fill the silence.

"Just couldn't."

"Nothing in particular kept you up?"

"Nope."

And that's going to be my answer, because there is no way I'm going to tell him that spending the morning with his family yesterday is what kept me awake. How they all know each other's day-to-day, how they all make it a point to meet weekly, how they all live in the same town and love being around each other.

The memories they could make felt endless.

I grab my phone to text my brother and grandma.

QUINN

Dinner this week.

I DEBATE USING a question mark but decide against it. I'm tired of asking to see my family. I need them to know I *want* to see them. So, I send a follow up text.

QUINN

Just tell me the day.

"WELL, I'll tell you what kept me up," Miles pulls me back into the conversation.

I put my phone in my purse and look at him. "What's that?"

"I found a dog in Wind Valley, and once they approve my application, I'm going to go get him."

"What? A real dog? I thought you were making that up. You're not just buying a dog to confirm our story, are you?"

He laughs at that. "I am not. I'm buying one because I always wanted one and I keep telling myself I'll get one, but I've never done the work to make it happen."

See, he's making things happen too. Taking charge isn't so bad.

"What kind of dog are we getting?" I ask.

"We," he says, "are adopting a golden retriever."

"That sounds like the perfect dog for us. What will we name—"

"Wait." Miles jerks his arm out in front of me to stop me before we open the door to B's Bakery.

I pause and look side to side, as if something happened that I can't see.

"What is it?"

"Look at the line."

I glance in the front window; Brooke has a longer line this morning. She does really well and this isn't anything new, but I love that the visitors of this town can see her gift as much as the locals.

Still, I'm not sure what exactly Miles is referring to at the moment.

"Is it too long? Do you want me to wait while you go back to the shop?"

The look he gives me says he really wants to roll his eyes right now, but he's powering through.

I grin.

"Don't," he says, because even in our short amount of time together, he can apparently read me well enough to know my next move. "Just look at the third and fourth person in line."

As nonchalantly as I can, I look into the window again.

The third person is Cherry and the fourth is Danny.

Oh.

"I'll come back later."

He sighs and then shakes his head. "No, we'll go in. I just didn't think we'd have to be the happy couple first thing in the morning."

"I think that's a chance we have to take in this town."

"Obviously."

I grab the door, and he groans, basically moving me out of the way so he can hold it for me instead of the other way around.

"I can open my own door, you know."

"I know, but it doesn't mean you should have to."

I lean in closer and whisper, "Look at you being a good boyfriend."

He lets out a low chuckle that catches Cherry's attention along with a couple of others in line.

She waves and smiles, her focus lasered in on Miles.

Her gaze only flickers to me before she turns back around in line.

Her movement must make Danny curious as to who just walked in, because now it's his turn to turn around.

"Quinn, hey," he says, smiling. He offers his hand to Miles. "Good to see you again, Miles."

"Yeah," Miles says but doesn't return the smile.

"Getting an early start for some big plans today?" Danny asks.

"No. We're just getting coffee and heading back to work," I answer.

Danny chuckles and shakes his head. "I still think it's crazy that you—"

He stops mid-sentence, his gaze colliding with Miles's. My fake boyfriend's arms are crossed as he glares at Danny.

"Never mind."

Danny turns back around.

I turn to give him my back and jerk Miles's arm down so that he's forced to bend and I can whisper in his ear.

"Was that called for?"

"Yes."

"Are you sure, because—"

"Oh my gosh, look at you two," Brooke says as she walks down the line of customers. Daisy is helping at the counter now. "Whispering all early in the morning. It's so cute, I could vomit."

"Morning, Brooke," Miles says.

"Morning," I add in a much cheerier tone than the grump next to me.

"You're here awfully early today. Was it a late night?" Brooke asks with a wink.

My cheeks blush. I pinch my lips to keep from laughing at how absurd her comment is, but I catch Cherry looking at me, and perhaps my attempt at not laughing is coming off as me hiding a smile for different reasons.

Cherry turns, her hair whipping behind her and hitting Danny in the face.

He steps back. "Whoa there, Red."

Cherry doesn't even give him the time of day. She just ignores him.

I glance at Miles to see if he saw that, too, but he's watching me.

His gaze is so intense that I instantly feel my stomach bottom out like I'm about to get in trouble.

Oh Jesus, what now?

This man is giving me whiplash. One minute we are all friendly on a leisure stroll for coffee, talking like besties, and now he won't take his eyes off me and is making sure people only say nice things to me.

I cannot keep up.

I pull my phone from my purse to see if my grandma or brother texted me back, but there are no notifications.

The line moves but slowly.

Before I know it, Miles and I are on our way back to the shop.

"Well, that definitely went a lot easier than I thought it was going to go."

I sip my coffee. "Did it?" I ask, letting my tone stand in as an eye roll.

"Are you sure you're telling me everything with Danny? He seems like a tool, and I don't like the backhanded comments he gives you."

"I did, yes. He is a nice guy, despite the impression he's given you."

Danny never spoke to me that way before. My guess is that he's doing it now because the sight of me with someone else stings. It's not an excuse, nor does it justify his behavior the last couple of days, but I have no other idea as to why he would act this way.

Miles sighs.

When he doesn't say anything for a moment, I steal a glance in his direction.

He's watching me.

"What?" I ask.

"Nothing."

"Oh, it's something if you're looking at me like that."

"Like what?"

"Like you don't even know what to think."

"I don't."

"About what?"

"You."

I grin.

"Well, just ask me something that will help ease your mind

so you can focus on work instead of thinking of me all day long."

He guffaws.

"I won't be thinking of you all day long."

"You might now."

"I won't," he says quickly, as if that's the end of the discussion.

"How many more times do you think we'll run into them in town like this?"

"A lot more."

"I'm afraid you might be right, and unless we want to have many more super fun and awkward moments like that, we need to knock this thing up a notch to get the point across. If we make them think we are absolutely lovesick, maybe they will avoid us. Cherry especially. Or we could set her up with someone."

"I see where your mind is going with this, but the only options are another local, and I'm not letting that happen, or a tourist, and I don't think we will get that lucky. We know—"

"Danny!" I shout before he can finish.

"What?"

"Let's set her up with Danny."

Miles stops.

"Whoa, who said anything about setting them up?"

"Me. It's perfect. You know her, and I know him."

"I don't know her, Quinn. We made out like teenagers maybe three times. That's it."

"Seriously?" My shoulders drop.

"I would have thought by her behavior that you gave her the best night of her life with those killer listening skills of yours, and now she can't get you out of her mind. Damn. Like a whole summer of bedroom fun."

He shivers. "I'm glad I cut it off before it could get that far."

"Well, I think this could still work."

"What?"

"Oh my gosh, Miles, keep up. We're setting Cherry up with Danny."

"We are not doing any such thing."

"We are."

"Quinn."

"Miles," I mock him. "It's happening."

"It's really not. Now I'm going to get back to work and so are you, and I do not mean forming a plan that involves Cherry or Danny or me or you."

I roll my eyes as he walks off, and a text comes in at the same time.

TOBIAS

Wednesday works for us. Bring Miles.

I GRIN and head to the office.

I don't care that I have to bring Miles—I'm just excited that I have plans with my family.

And I'm even more thrilled that I have a plan to help Miles avoid Cherry once and for all. He might not have thought this far ahead, but even after we fake break up, what's to say she won't come back next summer and try this all over again.

Nope. I have a plan to make this separation last.

I just need to get him on board with it first.

CHAPTER ELEVEN

MILES

Today was a good day.

I got an early start, which was nice even if it did include that hiccup at the bakery.

I mean, seriously, what are the chances?

High, it seems.

I think this is just how my life is supposed to be at this point. One giant obstacle after the next. Challenge after challenge.

It pisses me off, but somehow, I always seem to push through.

But there is no way in hell I'm playing matchmaker for the woman I'm trying to avoid.

I've agreed to a lot of stupid things with Quinn since this thing started. I have to draw the line somewhere.

Setting my ex, if you want to call her that, up with Quinn's ex, if we want to call him that, is a hard no.

Pass.

Not happening.

No way.

I lock the shop door and head for my house, ready for a hot

shower and to watch some mindless TV as I unwind for the night.

"Finally," Quinn says the moment she spots me walking past the apartment patio. "I was about five minutes from marching into the shop and demanding you quit working for the night so we can make a plan."

I keep walking but let my gaze run over her quickly. She's wearing that white flower pajama set again. Her hair is pulled back, and she's already removed her makeup for the night. The other times I've seen her in this outfit, she has bare feet, but tonight she's wearing white slip-on sneakers as she quickly follows behind me.

Also different from the other times is the six-pack of beer in one hand and the notebook with a pen in the other.

"If you're talking about a plan to set Cherry up with Danny, I stand by my answer from earlier."

I jog up the steps to my house, yanking on the door and holding it open for her. Quinn brushes past me as if she comes here frequently, walking right into the kitchen. She takes two beers from the carton and places the rest in the fridge.

Sure, by all means, just walk around like you own the place.

She locks her gaze on mine and then walks right up to me.

"Drink this."

I take the bottle and hold it up, examining it closer to the light.

"Did you put something in it?" I ask.

"No, but I'm going for the hope that you'll be a little more agreeable after a few of these."

I nod slowly, scratching my nose to hide my smile.

The look she's giving me is serious, as if what we plan to do here tonight is going to change everything.

Which it could if I agreed to it, but I didn't, and I've never really been the kind of guy who lucks out that easily.

Hence how we even got into this situation that has turned into a domino effect of stupid shit.

I honestly have no other way to explain it.

I twist the top off my beer and move toward the stairs, my stomach growling. "I'm going to take a quick shower, and then I'm going to sit on my couch and relax."

"Perfect. I'll go get some snacks."

She moves with purpose right back out the front door, and I laugh as I walk up to my bathroom.

When she sets her mind to something, she goes all in. The only reason I didn't tell her to forget about it again is because I'm curious about these snacks.

I skipped dinner.

I'm hungry.

I quickly shower and head back down to the living room in just a pair of sweats. I'll be honest, I debated putting a shirt on and chose not to. I'm not trying to start anything or show off the body I've put a lot of work into, like some cocky dipshit. I'm in my house, and this is how I'd be whether or not Quinn was here. If I have to sit here and argue over whether we should plan matchmaking, whatever you want to call it, for a woman I'm trying to avoid, I'm going to be as comfortable as I can get.

Quinn lets herself back in and marches right back into the kitchen.

"I decided to just make you a late dinner. When I was in Italy last summer, I signed up for this class to learn how to cook different pasta dishes, and it was incredible. I can make a fettuccine alfredo that will make you cry a lot faster than you think. Lucky for you, I was going to cook this tomorrow, so the noodles I made this afternoon while I was waiting for you to get off are ready."

That sounds delicious.

She sets the bags of ingredients down and then turns.

She pauses, her gaze directed solely on my chest.

I wait for her to make some kind of remark, a quick come-back to get my blood pumping.

"Do you need another beer?"

I chuckle and then cross my arms. "No, I haven't finished my first one yet, and you need to chill out. I know why you're here. No need to butter me up with beer and Italian food."

"Okay. I guess I won't cook."

"I didn't say that," I retort quickly. "You said pasta, and now I want pasta."

She rolls her eyes then as she starts talking a mile a minute about different places in town we could go, things we can do, and conversations we can help them engage in.

She is aware that I said I didn't want to help, right?

It's all a bit much for me, so it's time to move this conversation along.

"Why don't we just introduce them and let them take it from there?" It's an easy out and common sense.

She drops the wooden spoon into the sauce and spins, her hands on her hips. Clearly, my assumptions are wrong.

"Just introduce them? How will they have a meet-cute?"

"A what?"

"A meet cute."

"What the fuck is a meet-cute?"

I lean my hips on the counter next to where she's preparing the noodles. I cross one ankle over the other, sip my beer, and wait for her answer.

"It's the most important part of how two people meet, that first moment they notice each other. It sets the tone for their entire relationship."

"What's ours?"

"We don't have one, Miles, obviously."

"So, it's just for people who date?"

"Well, no."

"Then we probably have one. What is it?"

She thinks for a moment, then goes back to stirring the sauce. "I suppose in our situation, we could have different ones. Do you remember the first time you saw me or met me?"

"No," I lie quickly.

I've never told a soul the ice cream story, and I don't plan to change that today.

"Well, the first time I saw you was when Tobias wanted to go to a hockey game in Wind Valley. I was visiting, and he begged Grandma Betty to take us."

"Really?" I ask and take a sip of the beer she brought.

"Yep. He talked mostly about Hudson and how he was convinced he would go to the pros, but he pointed out you, Luca, a little girl, and your dad."

There are only a few times I recall the four of us being together at one of Hudson's games, and that was the season after our mom died. It was Hudson's last year; he'd already lined up a scholarship for college. Dad wanted us to get as much time together as possible.

The crazy part is that it was the same year I first saw Quinn.

I clear my throat. "Is that a meet cute?"

"No." She laughs. "I guess not, since we didn't even talk."

"So, ours is the first time we talked? Wasn't that … when you were talking to yourself on your phone down by the lodge?"

She adds the noodles and then moves to stand on my other side, mirroring my pose.

"Funny." She smirks. "I was doing a live show on Instagram, and you ruined it."

"I did not ruin it."

"Um, I recall you asking your brother who the weirdo was. Everyone watching heard you."

I smile. "Whoops."

"Anyway, we need to stage something like that for Cherry and Danny, but way better."

She comes up with more ideas as we eat. I nod, but I'm not really paying attention. I'm too busy trying to figure out how I'm going to get her to cook for me for the rest of the summer.

Maybe there could be some perks to having a fake girlfriend.

When we finish eating, I grab a couple more beers and move us into the living room to relax, but she's still talking.

"Jesus, Quinn. How do you have so much energy? Take a breath."

I sit on my couch, lean back, and watch her pace in front of me.

She needs to relax. Find something else to think about. Like me, for example. I could be annoyed that she's still talking about this, but instead, I'm focusing on her smooth skin. How those fucking legs of hers are actually in my house. In my living room. Just inches away.

How pissed would she be if I touched her? If I pulled her toward me until she dropped into my lap, one leg resting on each side of me?

I don't think she'd be pissed at all. If her reaction that first day in my shop had a say, I think she'd like it.

I bet her mind would calm down real quick.

"Oh my gosh, Miles, please pay attention. We need to have a plan."

"No, we don't. We can wing it."

"We are not going to just *wing* it, but I'm glad to hear you're finally on board with this. This is going to take a lot of brain power to pull this off, and we need—"

"Holy smokes, someone is wound tight."

I smile and shake my head. She's really worked up about this.

"I am not wound tight," she snaps.

"I beg to differ. I've been listening to you for the last half hour, Quinn."

"O-kay, it's official. We both have very different versions of listening, and you could use a refresher course on what that—"

"I bet I could touch you, slowly slide my hand between your thighs, and the moment I pressed a finger against you, you'd combust. That's how wound tight you are."

I freeze with my beer halfway to my mouth.

Where the fuck did that come from? Did I really just say that to her? It's one thing to let my mind wander, but to let those thoughts just slip from my lips so freely…

I quickly touch the bottle to my mouth and take a long pull, doing my best to pretend like the words that just flowed out of my mouth were as natural as me asking about the weather.

"I would not—you know what? I'm above this. I just wanted to make this easier for us, but clearly, you don't have any interest in making our lives easier. This summer or the summers after."

Hell, she has a point.

She stands quickly, clearly ready to leave. So I grab her hand. "Wait."

She stops, crossing her arms to look at me.

I drop my hand from hers, letting it fall back to the couch.

On the way, my fingers skim her bare leg.

I bet I could touch you, slowly slide my hand between your thighs, and the moment I pressed a finger against you, you'd combust.

Fuck. How long has it been since I've hooked up with someone who wasn't my hand?

Too fucking long if my brain and mouth have decided to just randomly reveal what we're thinking without debating the consequences first.

I brace myself for the argument I know is about to happen, but all I'm greeted with is silence.

After I pull myself together enough to look up, I find Quinn watching me. Her tongue sweeps out over her lips, and her gaze flickers from my eyes to my mouth.

No. Don't do that. Don't look at me like that.

We spend one night drinking beers and hanging out alone, and suddenly, this new tension shows up.

Hell, it's not new. We're just behind closed doors now, so it's heightened.

Fuck.

Me.

"I … I wouldn't," she finally says and steps back.

She wouldn't what? I can't remember what we were talking about.

I know the words didn't come out of my mouth, but she still finds a way to read them on my face.

"Combust," she says with more confidence now. "I would not combust from just one touch. Especially not from you."

I can't help but smirk. I might not have meant to say those words out loud, but going by her flushed cheeks right now and the way her words sound all breathy, I'd say I was right.

"If you say so."

I try not to reveal my smirk as her eyes narrow the longer she stares at me. I shouldn't enjoy this. Not one bit. I just told her a mere twelve hours ago that she shouldn't let people talk to her the way she does and here I am, saying inappropriate words and wishing they were actions instead.

Suddenly, the scowl on her face fades and a grin takes over as she rests her hand on my chest.

"I'll come up with a plan and just fill you in later," she says sweetly, letting her hand slide across my bare skin as she heads for the door. "Oh, and my family wants us over for dinner later this week."

She practically slams the door on the way out.

I touch the spot where her hand just was, my body on fire from one simple touch.

Part of me wishes she hadn't left, and I don't know how to feel about that.

New office assistant, check. Stack of applications for the shop position, check. Invoices sent to happy customers, check. Shop life is going smoother than usual; check. Does Quinn officially know she's controlling my summer—check, check, and check.

Only six more weeks to go.

I can do this.

Everything is going to be fine.

CHAPTER TWELVE

QUINN

I'm not okay.

It's been two days since I marched my happy self into Miles's house and demanded that he help me set Cherry up with Danny and two days since his hand touched my leg. My thigh. My outer thigh.

Touched.

Grazed.

Skimmed.

It doesn't matter what word I use, the moment our skin touched, it was like something had happened. An electric current of some kind and it sounds so stupid that I can't even say it out loud. I feel silly even thinking about it.

One touch isn't supposed to do this to me. One touch isn't supposed to cause me to lose my mind. One touch shouldn't make me question whether I should kiss my fake boyfriend. And one touch sure as hell shouldn't have me reach into my bedside drawer to relieve the tension that damn thigh graze caused.

We arrived at Grandma Betty's house about thirty minutes

ago, and she's been talking nonstop since we got here to Miles about her first car.

Natalie and Tobias are sitting on the floor doing tummy time with the twins, and I'm just watching it all, while also letting my mind run wild over what should be nothing.

"So, what do you two have planned for this summer?" Tobias asks as he coos at baby Dixon.

"Please tell us—I need to live vicariously through you for the next couple of months," Natalie adds.

"Just hanging out," I say as calmly as I can.

Definitely just hanging out and not anything more.

Even though it's been a while since a man touched me, and perhaps it wouldn't be the worst thing.

Then again, we all know how my last fling ended, and I can't go through that again.

At the same time, Miles refuses to commit to anyone who doesn't plan to settle down here, so we'd be on the same page, right?

I drop my head back on the chair and sigh. Why am I even thinking about this? It's not an option.

"Oh, please tell me you're doing more than just hanging out," Natalie whines. "This"—she points to the twins—"is what happens when you just 'hang out' alone."

I gasp as if that's completely absurd. "Oh, that's not …we—"

"I beg you not to finish," Tobias says and gets up. "I'm going into the kitchen to see if Miles needs rescuing from Grandma B."

He pauses to kiss Natalie's forehead and then he's gone.

"Have you two not had sex?" Natalie asks immediately.

"That's your first question about our relationship?"

She rolls her eyes and smiles. "Look at him, Quinn."

"Oh, I know what he looks like, Natalie."

Oh god, do I. With and without a shirt.

"So, he's the one who wants to wait?"

"We," I start to say, but I can't come up with anything fast enough. "Yes. He wants to take it slow."

Have you ever known a person who didn't like you or who only tolerated you? Then you find yourself in a situation where you make it worse, but at the same time, is it really worse if they didn't like you to begin with. No? Just me?

"That's kind of sexy," Natalie whispers.

"Way," I agree.

"Way what?" Grandma Betty joins us in the living room. I glance behind her, but the guys aren't with her. "They went to look at Mike's Harley in the garage."

"Should he still be driving a Harley?" I ask.

"Yes." The look my grandmother gives me could kill, and I almost laugh at how quickly she answered me. "Now, what are we talking about?"

"Oh, just how Mike seems to take more risks than Miles," Natalie says with a laugh.

"Nat," I scold and then cover my face.

Maybe I could tell these two the truth. They won't tell anyone, will they? I mean, they are family. Maybe I could even get Tobias on board with this whole thing.

"Well, risk or not, I'm thrilled over this. Does it mean you'll stay in Lovers longer than just a summer? My grandma heart says, 'Don't get your hopes up,' but they are high, my dear."

Well, so much for telling her the truth.

"I … I'm not sure what it means."

"Well, haven't you two talked about it?"

"Of course." I lean back and cross my arms. "It's a sensitive subject."

"I'll bet it is," Grandma adds. She picks up Nina and bounces her on her hip toward the kitchen.

Natalie hands me Dixon, then stretches her legs out.

"Whatever you two decide, don't let anyone guilt you into

anything, okay? The best things take time. Look at me and your brother."

"I don't think it's going to take Miles and I ten years to figure this out."

Less than ten weeks together actually, but those are details Natalie doesn't need to know.

"I'll bring it by next week. Thank you, Miles," Mike says as they all file out of the kitchen and into the living room.

"Bring what by?" I ask Miles.

He scratches the back of his neck. "His Harley. The fuel tank is acting up, so I told him I'd look at it."

"You don't have time on your schedule for that."

"I'll make time."

"Now, now." Grandma Betty marches into the room. "Don't be doing my fiancée any favors if it means taking away time from my granddaughter. I need you to keep her absolutely smitten—that way she never wants to leave Lovers again."

Miles meets my eyes over the top of the baby Dixon's head.

I give him a half smile, and he mirrors it.

First his dad and now Grandma Betty. We didn't take the effect this would have on our loved ones into consideration.

"Is everything all set up for the ceremony?" I ask quickly to change the subject. This specific question sends Grandma into a frenzy where she starts to share all the details. As she talks, my gaze falls to the fireplace, where a wedding photo of Natalie and my brother sits, then it drifts to a shot of the twins propped against it, waiting for the frame my grandmother has yet to purchase for it.

I scan the mantle over her fireplace. There is one of her and Mike, more of Natalie and Tobias, and a couple of my parents. At the end is a picture of me. Alone.

I remember when she took it. It was a good day. We were at one of the many festivals that Lovers has, and I won a gift basket filled with random goodies the town is known for. There were books, baked goods, a gift certificate for the spa at Lovers Lodge, and a few other knickknacks.

I'd bet Tobias I would win it, and I was smiling so big because, as his sister, I still love when I'm right instead of him.

Yet right now, looking at the photo makes me sad.

I take in all the other pictures around the room, and one by one, memories come back to me. Weddings, graduations, birthdays.

It's like having your life surrounding you.

Will I ever have a room like this?

Maybe my life is ready to go in a different direction.

There is more to life than traveling, I know that, but what does that life look like for me?

———

"LET'S do this again next week," Grandma Betty says as Miles and I step out the door. "I loved having a full house, and I need more of it."

She hugs Miles and then me. "Good night, dear. I love you."

"I love you, too," I say as we follow her sidewalk to the street.

"Hudson and Sadie invited us to Hudson's for a drink. Do you want to go?" Miles asks.

"You're willingly inviting me to hang out with you?"

He chuckles.

"Well, it'll be nice to not have to pretend for a bit. Although, to be honest, your family seems just as laid back as mine."

"If you don't count the part where they make us feel guilty."

Miles sighs. "Yeah, I picked up on that, too."

"Do you think we're just being ... immature about this? I

mean, we're adults, so shouldn't we just suck it up and break up now so we can deal with the consequences?"

"We both know this was a stupid idea, Quinn, but it's working. Cherry isn't showing up at the bar, and that's worth all this hassle for me."

I nod. "You definitely have more at stake than I do. I just have my pride on the line."

"Pride is important."

"I just … Grandma Betty seemed so hopeful tonight that I feel like a bad person."

"I get it. My dad seemed relieved that you came into my life. Like I wasn't happy or something and now that I have you, maybe I could be."

"Oh, I don't think he thought you were unhappy."

"Yeah, you're probably right, but it still feels that way sometimes."

We walk most of the way in silence. I'm not sure what he's thinking, but I gave him an out and he didn't take it.

Sure, it's because he wants to keep Cherry away, but he could have changed his mind.

As soon as Miles opens the door to the bar, Hudson bombards us.

"Did you see my text?"

"No." Miles reaches into his pocket for his phone. He scans his messages quickly. "Fuck."

"What?" I ask.

"Everyone is here right now."

"Everyone, as in …"

"As in, it's time to be the doting girlfriend."

"Doting girlfriend?" I repeat. "The most we've had to do is stand in line shoulder to shoulder at the coffee shop and hang out at our families' homes. There has been no doting. What does that even look like?"

"Like you are obsessed with him," Hudson says in a clear and specific tone. "You're on."

"On wha—"

"Quinn, Miles, this is perfect," Sully walks up. "We just ordered a round of drinks. We'd love for you to join us."

Sully nods over his shoulder to where Andy, Danny, and Ashley are sitting. A few of their other friends are with them, but I don't know their names. I only recognize them from photos online. Everyone is grouped up in pairs, except Danny.

Well, this should be fun.

"You know, we would love to," Miles says and then swings his arm over my shoulders. "But we were really just stopping in to see my brother real fast. We don't plan to stay."

"Just one drink. I won't pressure you for more. We just … Andy would like to get to know you. We haven't seen Quinn in almost a year."

"Oh, we—"

"One drink, that's it," Miles cuts me off.

"Great. Go do whatever it is you came here for and meet us at our table."

Sully jogs off to take a seat by Andy.

"Why did you say yes?" I ask.

"Because I have a hunch they will ask us this same thing anytime they see us out until we say yes. If I say yes now, we can get it over with."

"I see your point."

"Let's get our drinks first."

Miles grabs my hand, pulls me to the bar, and places our order with Hudson.

"What's your plan now?" Hudson asks, leaning onto the counter. He's playing the part that we came to see him about something and he doesn't even know it.

"No clue. Pray for the best, I guess," Miles says.

"We'll be fine. It's the same as any other time, but maybe put your arms around me again, and please make sure I'm not sitting by Danny."

Miles nods.

"I have an idea," Hudson says. We turn to him with the eagerness of a toddler who was promised candy for doing the smallest task. "What if you go to the extreme?"

"The extreme. What does that mean?" I ask.

"Be so into each other that it makes them sick. Be so touchy and cringy that they don't want to hang out with you ever again."

Miles stands tall with his hands on his hips.

"Maybe I just tell them, 'Sorry, no can do, because I want to get her home and naked as soon as possible.' That's cringy, right?"

I swat his arm.

"You are not saying that."

"But it's cringy. It felt cringy as I was saying it."

Hudson leans in close to Miles's face.

"What?" He leans back.

"That shit just fell from your mouth sounding a lot like Luca, so I was checking."

"Fuck off."

Is this what happens to Miles when he's nervous?

Ugh. We don't have time for him to be nervous right now.

"I hate to admit this, but I think Hudson's idea has merit. Not enough for you to tell them how badly you want to get me naked, but yeah, I think it would work."

"Just kiss after everything the other one says, and I bet they leave in under five minutes," Hudson offers.

"No thanks, I will not be kissing her."

My head jerks back.

"Excuse me. That was a bit rude, and the response was a bit too quick for my liking."

"Do you want me to kiss you?"

"No," I answer quickly, but in the back of my mind, I start to think otherwise.

I glance at his lips.

I mean, it wouldn't be the worst.

Especially after I spent the better part of the last two days obsessing over how he touched me.

Clearly, that was one-sided. I hate the pit that forms in my stomach at his rejection. I hold my head and laugh it off.

"Let's go," I say, letting Miles scramble to follow behind me.

Good. Look like a lovesick puppy following me around. *You deserve it after that kiss comment.*

"Yay, sit!" Andy gestures to the chair next to her. The chair. Singular.

"There is room here, too," Danny says, pointing at the open spot next to him.

As my brain processes the polite way to ask Danny to move to the chair so Miles and I can sit on the couch, Miles brushes past me and drops himself into the chair. Then he smacks his thigh.

"Babe, sit."

Babe.

Sit.

Is he serious right now?

"Oh, I—" I see Danny grinning and scooting over. "I'd love to."

Miles has the audacity to look shocked at my response, so I cup his face as I sit and whisper into his ear, "Smile."

"I can't believe you just did that," he whispers back.

To the people around us, we probably look like two lovesick kids nuzzling each other's necks, but that is far from the truth.

"We are supposed to look like we like each other."

"No, we are supposed to look like we're obsessed with each other."

"Oh, look at you two." Andy sighs. "I'm just so happy that you found someone."

I turn to face everyone, letting my back rest against Miles. He adjusts his legs to hold my weight, and his hand moves to my front to steady me. His palm rests flat with his fingers stretched wide over my stomach, causing me to suck in a breath.

His hand is so big that his thumb rests right between my breasts and his pinky is touching the hem of my shorts.

That's ... a big hand.

On another breath, I glance down and then close my eyes.

Yep, that is a big hand with thick fingers, and why the heck am I thinking about his fingers?

I focus on my breathing as I smile at everyone while they talk about the wedding.

Miles leans forward, his chest fitting flush to my back.

"Doing okay there, *Quinny*?" he whispers in my ear.

I nod.

"Are you sure? I can feel you breathing."

The warmth of his breath skirts over my skin, causing me to break out into goosebumps.

Hell, why am I reacting like this? He's clearly not interested in me like that.

And why would he be? This is all fake.

It's fake.

It's fake.

It's fake.

"You do realize I have a front row seat to your body right now. The way you breathe, the way you shiver, the way you keep leaning into me when I talk. I think what I said the other night is even more spot-on right now with you in my lap."

I grab my drink and take a sip.

"So it's settled. You're coming," Andy says.

Beer sprays from my mouth, all over Ashley.

"I'm so sorry," I say, standing quickly. "I'll get a towel."

Miles jerks me back, keeping me in place.

"Hudson is already walking over here with one."

"Good," Ashley snaps. "What is wrong with you?"

Andy giggles, and Danny's watching Miles with annoyance.

Hudson helps wipe down the table after telling Ashley where to find the bathroom. "I think," Andy says, "Miles was whispering sweet nothings into Quinn's ear."

"I was," he says with confidence. "It's hard not to when someone this beautiful is sitting on your lap. I mean, if I had it my way, we would be back at home and—"

"Okay, time to go." I spring up again, chug the rest of my beer.

"See what I mean." Miles chuckles but stands with me. "See you all around."

With that, he places his hand on my lower back and pushes me toward the door.

As soon as we are outside, he pulls his hand away.

"I told you my idea would work. Look how fast we got out of there," he says and starts to walk faster. It's annoying. "Now put some pep in your step so that we don't get pulled into another—"

"Wait!" Andy calls out. "We wanted to invite you hiking this Thursday. It would be great if you could come with us. Since you know the area."

Hiking, again?

Miles scratches the back of his neck.

"Hey, Miles," a high-pitched voice says behind us.

Cherry.

"Oh, hey." He takes a step closer to me. And because I'm not a dick, even though I'm extra annoyed with him right now, I lace my fingers with his.

Andy waves at Cherry but doesn't move. She's waiting for a response, after all.

"Thursday is a busy day for us," I say. "Maybe a different day."

"Friday?" Andy suggests.

"Friday for what?" Cherry asks.

Now, normally, I'd be thinking how rude that she just engaged herself in our conversation, but right now I'm not normal Quinn. I'm matchmaker Quinn.

I smile big.

"We are all going hiking—would you want to come with our group?"

Ouch.

Fuck.

Fuck.

My hand.

Why is he squeezing it so hard?

I try to pull away, but Miles just jerks me closer and wraps a hand around my waist. He pulls me close as if he were about to kiss my cheek.

"What the fuck are you doing?" he whispers.

"Trust me," I say just as quietly.

I resume my smile in Cherry's direction. "Next Friday works for us if it works for you."

"Oh, um, I don't know. I don't know any of you but Miles," Cherry says quickly.

"I'm Andy." Andy offers her hand. "I'm getting married at the end of the summer and I used to travel a lot with Quinn. I can share my social media with you, and you can check me out before you decide, but the more the merrier."

Cherry eyes her cautiously.

"Are you going?" she asks, her question directed at Miles.

He nods. "Yes, Quinn and I will be there."

I can hear the pain in his voice, and I smile even bigger.

"Okay, maybe. Yeah, that could be fun."

"Great!" I say a little too cheerily. "See you on Friday."

"I'll text you with the details," Andy says. "Want to come inside, Cherry, and meet my fiancé and his brother?"

Cherry agrees, but she seems reluctant. As they turn to the bar, she looks over her shoulder one last time, so I pretend I don't notice and kiss Miles's cheek.

It was a risky move.

I gave him no warning, and yet he didn't pull away.

Weird.

After the comment he made, I thought it would be the opposite.

"Are they gone?" he asks.

"Yep."

As soon as that one word is out of my mouth, he steps back, making sure not one piece of our bodies are left touching.

"Let's go home before we make this any worse," he says.

I follow behind him, because although yes, that was a mess, I can't help but smile.

If this Cherry and Danny plan works, then no more faking and we can go back to normal.

Normal.

My smile falls.

Is that what I want?

CHAPTER THIRTEEN

MILES

The sun is shining with a slight breeze, and not a cloud in sight.

It's the perfect day for a hike. Yet, I'm still annoyed about it.

I've been annoyed since the moment Quinn agreed to do this last week. And then invited Cherry along, no less.

The whole point of this was to get Cherry to leave me alone, yet now I'm making plans with her.

Fuck.

"I cannot believe I let you talk me into this," I say in a hushed, clipped tone as I lean down to Quinn. "I have done an obscene number of stupid things this summer since you showed up and it's only been, what? Maybe three weeks."

I shake my head, continuously disappointed with myself, while Quinn rolls her eyes.

"Everything is going to be fine. Just remember why we are doing this."

I remember just fine, and that's the problem. If this works the way Quinn thinks it will, all will be good, and I will happily take back every rude comment of doubt I've made to her. If this doesn't work, then we just look like idiots.

She'll leave and not think twice about it. I'll still be here listening to everyone in town talk about that one time I pretended to date the pretty traveler girl.

Who, as it turns out, is a lot more than just the traveler girl.

It's just easier if I keep her that way in my head.

I glance over at the rest of our hiking crew. Andy and Sully are stretching as if the leisure hike we are about to take is going to be a sprint. Their other blonde friend didn't want to come, and Cherry is playing on her phone while Danny ties his shoes. The two of them are sharing a rock as a chair, so that's a start, right?

Maybe this is a sign I need to take a breath and just go with the flow.

Then again, a better sign would be if they were talking.

God, I can't believe I'm doing this.

How am I not learning that my choices have consequences?

One day I'm working in the shop with a schedule that won't quit and a quiet life, and now I'm fake dating a travel influencer and trying to set the woman who is obsessed with me up with another man.

What the fuck happened to me?

"Are you growling?" Quinn asks with wide eyes.

"No."

"It sure sounded like it."

"I didn't growl. I'm annoyed."

"You're always annoyed. What's a girl got to do to make you smile?"

My mouth opens to reply, but she holds a finger up, pressing it to my lips. I know it shouldn't, but the gentle pressure sends my mind racing over how gentle she'd be in other … actions.

"Don't answer that."

I chuckle as her lips tug to a smile.

I'm annoyed that I enjoy the banter Quinn and I have with

each other. She's quick with her comebacks, and I like it. Maybe a little too much, and I don't want to like it.

Don't even get me started on my brother mentioning kissing last week.

I panicked so fast. My only other option was for them to see how much I did want it.

Ever since she stood in my living room and glanced at my lips, I've thought about it.

I know Quinn well enough that it wouldn't be weird, but I don't know her well enough to be thinking about her lips obsessively.

Which is what I've been doing. How naturally dark pink they are. How plump they are. How smooth they look.

Oh, hell.

Luckily, the two of us have been doing our best to just work and lay low. Until now, we haven't put ourselves in another position to touch or pretend we don't want to kiss. Or at least, pretend I don't. Does she?

Why am I thinking about this right now?

I should be thinking about work or, better yet, at work. But fuck, she's got that so organized that taking this afternoon off didn't even seem like it would affect anything.

She's been helping me in so many ways, I should just man up and help her right now.

I'm starting to think that admitting the truth, although it might have sucked at first, would have been a lot easier to deal with.

Too fucking late now.

"Look how close they are," Quinn says, nodding toward Cherry and Danny. "This might be easier than I thought."

She stands, having finally finished lacing her hiking boots. She's wearing long foam-green leggings with dark brown hiking boots, her white socks sticking out of the top. She's got on a skintight tank top that matches her leggings and a light jacket tied around her waist. As she stands with her back to the sun, the light makes her brown hair, which is braided down her back, look almost blonde.

"Ready?"

I nod, looking down at my attire.

Jeans, shirt, hiking boots.

Simple.

Quinn and I couldn't be more different.

Jesus. Are people really buying this? The more I think about it, the more I wonder.

"Great," she says and then walks toward the others. My eyes drift to her ass; her sweater is a little off to the side, revealing one perfectly round bubble cheek.

I see her ass a lot when she's in her pajama shorts, but something about the way her leggings hug her every curve buzzes my body to life.

She looks over her shoulder and winks.

Well, I take it that's my clue to get into boyfriend mode.

I stride up behind her and sling my arm around her shoulders.

"Let's do this," I say.

"Yes, but first, everyone get a buddy," Quinn announces like she's the leader of the group. "Andy and Sully, me and Miles, Cherry and Danny. Does that work for everyone?"

A collective group of yeses takes place.

I turn to start the hike.

Quinn might know where to go, but a perk of growing up in Lovers is knowing these trials like the back of my hand.

I make it about four steps before Quinn reaches for my arm. Her small fingers loop around my bicep as she picks up her pace to meet me step for step. She leans in close, and we fall into stride.

"I thought we could stay in the back. It would make it easier for me to fake an injury."

She glances over her shoulder to smile at the group behind us.

I don't slow my pace, but I do walk closer to her so that I can whisper, "That's your great plan?"

She nods. "Yes, it is. Then you have to take me away—far, *far* away—to get the care I need."

I have no words.

Fake an injury. That is her grand plan.

Fuck.

I'm stuck on this stupid hike from beginning to end.

"So, how did you two start dating?" Andy asks behind us.

"The apartment behind his shop was vacant, and I needed a place to stay. I kind of wore him down until he had no choice," Quinn says calmly.

"And then you just started working for him?" Sully follows up.

"Pretty much. Miles works a lot, maybe too much, and it made sense that he get a little help."

"I still think it's crazy that you two didn't really get along and then all of the sudden you're dating," Cherry says, her comment coming out of nowhere.

"You two haven't always been friendly?" Danny asks.

Shit. Shit. Shit.

"No," Cherry answers for us.

I cast a glance at Quinn, whose eyes meet mine as she scrunches her nose.

"Everyone in this town knows that Quinn and Miles never got along until this summer," Cherry goes on. "In fact, one rumor I heard was that Miles used to avoid, sometimes even leave, places because she showed up. Apparently now, he's smitten with her."

I close my eyes and drop my chin to my chest.

She's not wrong.

I wouldn't do it now, of course, but I've done it in the past.

The way Cherry says it makes me sound like a dick. Which I am, or was, but I didn't always do it in the way they are all thinking.

I chance a glance at Quinn, but her head is down as she keeps walking.

The not caring for her part isn't new information to Quinn, but the fact that I used to leave places is.

I clear my throat. "Things changed last summer near the end," I say, remembering that Quinn's friends think this has been going on since around that time. "Things are different now."

"Clearly," Cherry snaps.

"Do you come to Lovers often?" Danny asks her.

"My family and I have come here every summer for the last seven years."

"Oh, wow. It really is beautiful. What's your favorite part?"

I can't believe I'm saying this, but thank god for Danny and his smooth segue way to change the topic. Cherry is looking at him with confusion, but then she sighs and answers his question.

"I like that nothing here is rushed. City life can get crazy, and when I'm here, everything just seems simple."

Before we know it, Cherry and Danny are deep in conversation over places they've traveled and comparing trip secrets.

All in all, they seem to be hitting it off very well.

As for me, guilt is settling in.

I reach my hand out and rub Quinn's back. "Are you all right?"

"Mm-hmm."

"Are you sure?"

She nods.

I stop, reaching my hand out to grab hers and halt her as well.

"We'll catch up," I say to the others and point ahead of us. "When you get to a fork in the road, go right."

"Thanks." Sully beams and takes the lead.

Cherry and Danny walk right by us, chatting away.

I'm not even sure they know they passed us.

After they are out of hearing range, Quinn speaks first.

"Was she telling the truth?"

As much as I might want to, I don't try to deny it.

"Yeah."

The glint in her eyes hits me right in the heart.

Fuck. I think I made her cry.

"You really left places in your own hometown because I was there?"

I nod.

"Wow. You hate me that much?" She tosses her hands up and starts to hike again.

"Wait, no, I don't hate you. I never did, I just didn't know you, and whenever I was near you … I just … I—"

How do I explain this without making it seem like I've secretly been crushing on her all these years?

"You just what, Miles?"

"I just didn't understand you, and it pissed me off because I fucking wanted to."

She pauses to look at me.

"What?"

"You are everything the opposite of me, Quinn. It both scared and fascinated me, but at the end of the day, one thing never changed."

"What's that?"

"That you would leave. I never saw the point in us getting to know each other if you were going to keep leaving."

"Oh."

I run a hand through my hair.

"By the time I matured enough to realize how stupid that mindset was, I'd already sealed our relationship."

She doesn't say anything, but she also doesn't move, so I take that as a small sign that she isn't going to hold this against me.

"Do you want to get to know me now?" she asks.

I nod. "Isn't that what we've been doing since we started this?"

She shrugs. "A little. We've mostly been getting by to make everyone believe our story, but I don't think it's been the real us."

I smirk. "The real us, huh? I don't know if the real us is a good idea."

"There's only one way to find out." She winks.

"What's—"

"Ahhhh!" Quinn screams before I can finish. Then she drops to the ground. "Ahhhh!"

I squat to ask her what's wrong at the same time the group comes running back.

"What happened?"

"Are you okay?"

"You just scared the shit out of me."

"Quinn, what happened?"

The moment Quinn's eyes lock onto mine, I remember what she said.

It's showtime.

"She stepped wrong. I think she rolled her ankle."

"It hurts really bad," she says and reaches for my hand to squeeze it. "Oh, wow, it hurts."

"Let me look at it," I say. "Try not to move."

My intentions are to look like a doting boyfriend, but as my hand glides down her leg, I find myself thinking about a lot more than how to get out of this hiking day.

I slowly unlace her shoe, and a vision of her slowly unbuttoning one of those damn pajama shirts flashes into my mind.

Oh, hell. They aren't even the same thing, but it's turning me on all the same.

"Aren't boots like that made for this?" Cherry asks. Her tone is dry and deeply annoyed.

"Yeah," I respond quickly. "If you lace them correctly, and it looks like Quinn didn't."

"So it's her own fault," Cherry rolls her eyes. "Smart."

"Hey, I tried my best," Quinn argues, sending a glare in Cherry's direction and then in mine.

I hold back my smile.

"Either way, it looks like I'm going to have to cut this adventure short for us. You guys go on. I'll have Quinn give you an update later."

"Oh no, I'm sorry Quinny." Andy laces her fingers with Sully's. "Good thing we took a picture of the map at the lodge earlier. We'll be fine."

"Is it weird if I still tag along?" Cherry asks.

"No," Danny answers eagerly. "I hope you do."

Once we all say goodbye, Quinn and I wait once again for them to all be out of earshot.

"I can't believe faking an injury worked," I say. "It was kind of a pathetic show, to be honest."

She smacks my chest and stands.

"Yes, because your acting skills suck."

"I didn't pass that class while I was learning how to change a flat tire."

Quinn rolls her eyes.

"I can't believe how much Cherry and Danny bonded over you hating me."

I let out a breath of a laugh. "Are you going to forget that?"

"Nope," she says and starts to lace her boot back up. "Not a chance."

Figures.

She starts to head back down the trail.

"Who knows, maybe I'll use it against you when you break up with me, and by the looks of today, I just might be out of your hair before you know it."

I follow behind her in silence.

I don't really know what to say because the first thing that comes to mind shocks me.

Turns out, I like having her around, and knowing that we'd be fake breaking up before I really had the chance to know her bums me out.

CHAPTER FOURTEEN

QUINN

He used to leave places just because I was there.

Wow.

I didn't expect Cherry's words to hurt, but they did. It was like someone stuck the tiniest needle into my chest. It was sharp and quick, and the pain snuck up on me.

I shouldn't be upset about this, and I know he apologized, but I still can't stop thinking about it.

His explanation made sense, but I guess I wasn't aware of how much I affected him. We weren't even friends, but here I was coming into his hometown as if my presence meant nothing to these people when it did.

It does.

Miles pulls his truck into his driveway, pushing the button to turn it off.

Neither of us has spoken on the drive home, so when he unbuckles his seat belt, the click startles me. The noise basically jumpstarts me into motion.

"See you tomorrow," I say as I rush to get out and turn for the apartment.

"Quinn," Miles calls out, hurrying around the front of his truck.

I pause, turning slowly.

He's rubbing the back of his neck. A sign I've learned means whatever he's about to say next isn't easy for him.

"I'm going to take the rest of the night off, and I thought maybe you'd like to hang out."

Hang out? He wants to hang out … with me.

Not for show, but because he wants to.

"We could do something simple like order a pizza and then drink a few beers on my back porch."

He clears his throat as he waits for my answer. After our conversation on the mountain, getting to know each other seems to be the route we want to take, but now I'm a little nervous about it.

Do I want to hang with Miles Asher?

Of course, I do.

But he wasn't wrong with what he said earlier.

I'll leave at the end of the summer, so what's the point in getting to know each other better?

Knowing people for a short period of time is something I'm used to, but it's obvious that it's not something that appeals to Miles.

"Are you asking me because you feel bad for what was said earlier?"

His face shows zero expression as he thinks over his answer. I don't want him to invite me to come over just because he feels guilty.

"Yes and no." He steps closer to me. "I told you that by the time I grew up enough to decide it was stupid not to get to know someone just because they were leaving, I'd already created this thing between us. But I'm standing here right now asking you to give me the opportunity to change that."

Well, that was cute. I bite my lower lip to control the smile that wants to take over.

"Oh my god, Quinn, are you going to keep making me suffer waiting for an answer, or are we going to eat food and have some drinks?" He chuckles. "Because if we are doing this, you should know I'm not very patient, and admitting when I'm wrong isn't easy."

To that, I let my smile free.

"Jesus," he groans. "Just come on then."

I nod and move toward him. "If we are doing this," I say quietly, mimicking him, "then you should know I like it when certain people boss me around."

I hear the second groan as soon as I walk away. This one is different from the first one, though.

I like this one more.

———

"So you're saying that you honestly can't pick your favorite place to visit?" Miles asks as he leans back on the patio chair he's taking up. I'm in the one next to him.

"I know it's a common question, and most people have an instant answer, but I've been to far too many places to choose."

"Yeah." He sips his beer. "I suppose the average person has to think of—what, ten or fewer countries they've visited in their lifetime, which makes it easy to pick."

Last I checked, the average person visits eighteen countries in their lifetime, but the last thing Miles wants to hear is random traveling facts.

"Maybe, yeah. I'm not sure how they do it. How about you tell me your favorite place to go and then explain it to me."

"Oh, I'm the average person?"

"I mean," I say and hold both hands up. "That was the term you picked."

He chuckles, which in turn causes me to smile.

It's been like this for the last hour. Just easy conversation as we sit outside. To be honest, this right here would have to be a top contender to his question. The way the sun is setting, casting a purple and pink glow over the mountain and the lake below it is breathtaking. Not to mention the halo the colors provide over the lodge.

Gosh. If someone were getting married right now, this would be the perfect backdrop to have.

I snapped a couple of pictures of the view and posted them but didn't say where I was. If someone follows my page that closely, they'll know where I am.

Miles leans forward and grabs another slice of pizza. To my surprise, he didn't fight me on the cheese-stuffed crust and supreme toppings. It's nothing fancy or crazy, but the cheese-stuffed crust was something my grandma always did, so it felt fitting here.

His attention, like mine, falls to the view.

To be fair, I'm not so sure it's just the view that's winning me over right now.

The company definitely plays a role.

Turns out, when we're not fighting, we get along very well.

Maybe a little too well.

"Do you know where you're headed after Lovers?"

I grab my beer bottle and swirl the liquid as I think over the answer. Most people see only the travel side of my life—they don't see how it's also my job.

"I'll receive an email soon to let me know."

"An email?"

He couldn't hide the surprise on his face if he tried.

"Yep."

"You let someone else decide for you?"

"When they are paying me, yes." I let out a chuckle.

"What now?" he asks, turning to face me and ready to dive into the topic of my life. "This is going to sound stupid, but I thought you traveled for fun."

"Most people think that. And at times I do, but most of the travel I do now is contracted. I travel, take pictures, and share their business or whatever they need on my accounts, and they pay me for it."

"That's a real job?"

I hold my hands up. "It's mine."

He studies me for a moment.

"So your on-the-go-lifestyle isn't by choice?"

"It was at first, but now, it's because I signed paperwork that said I'd do whatever they needed."

"So even if you want to do something different …"

"I have contracts to fulfill."

He rubs his chin. "I don't know if I could do that. Not knowing what's next. I *always* know what's next. I like the structure and the routine. It makes me feel like I have control."

I nod. "I like those things, too, but it's different because my routine is not staying in one place too long and my structure is that I don't get too attached."

As soon as the words are out of my mouth, this weird feeling consumes me.

Sadness mixed with fear.

Is that what's wrong with me?

Do I not want that life anymore?

If I decide to change my career, I could lose everything. Where would that leave me?

What would I do to make money?

I clear my throat, nodding to the tire swing I've had my eye on since we sat down.

"I haven't been on one of these in years." I stand quickly, almost skipping all the steps as I put some distance between us.

I'm enjoying myself so much, and I don't want to keep bringing the vibe down by talking about leaving and where I'm going next because I don't know any of those things.

I take hold of the rope and put one leg at a time through the tire. Once I wiggle to a good spot, I start to kick my legs.

Forget the tire swing—I can't even remember the last time I went swinging at all.

The warm evening air brushes my face as I move faster.

God, even the swing is in a position to take in the view.

It's so peaceful.

"I think you might be the first person to actually use this," Miles says, stepping up next to the tire.

He leans against the tree, crosses his ankles and watches me.

I let out a laugh.

"Really? And here I thought you and your six-foot solid frame came out here nightly to have a little fun."

His head falls back on a chuckle. "Maybe I'll have to start."

"Or maybe I'll be over here hogging this spot all to myself. I mean, shoot, Miles, look at that view. I think I might be obsessed with it."

"Yeah," he says quietly. "It was actually one of the reasons I chose to build a house right behind the shop. It's not ideal, considering I had to make my own street, but this view was hard to pass up."

"I think it was the right choice."

"Me too."

I lean back, trying to get my legs to pump a little harder. Suddenly, Miles groans.

"Okay, first-timer, let me push you."

"No. I don't need help," I say a little too quickly.

The last thing I need right now is Miles touching me.

It's not often I get nights like this. One where I don't need to be anywhere but right here.

"Let's see how high this thing will go," he says right before he gives me the first shove.

I squeal and he laughs.

I come back down, and he pushes harder.

My grip tightens on the rope as I fly higher and higher with each push.

"I swear to god, Miles, if you push me so high that the rope breaks or I fall out, all the progress we made tonight will be gone."

I swing back to him.

"Poof," I say when his hand touches my back again. "Vanished."

As I come back down, he grabs the tire, jerking it to a stop and spinning it until he's standing in front of me.

"Well, we can't have that now, can we?"

His eyes lock onto mine for a split moment before they flash to my lips.

My heart instantly races.

Did he just think about kissing me?

We don't do that.

He doesn't do that.

He looks away quickly as if he's having the same internal conversation.

I let out a breath.

It's time for me to go. Two beers are enough for me to do something I shouldn't.

I start to pull my legs out in the most graceful way possible when Miles grabs the swing.

"Wait." One of his hands drops to my thigh.

My chest rises and falls quickly. He looks like he's at war with something now.

He licks his lips and then brings his other hand to my face, cupping my cheek and stroking my bottom lip with his thumb.

I think it's safe to say that kissing me is at the top of his mind, and if he chooses to do it, I'm not going to stop him. It might not be the best choice to make, but making bad choices seems to be our thing these days.

Then his hand drops from my face *and* from my leg.

"Thanks for coming over tonight," he says.

I only nod and force a smile.

He starts nodding, too, never taking his gaze off mine.

The tension in the way he looks at me is almost unbearable.

I break the connection and start to get out again, but Miles stops me again. This time both hands are on my face as he crashes his lips to mine.

His hands are so big that when he slides them back just an inch, his fingers are threading through my hair and gently tugging.

The action makes me moan, which causes him to deepen the kiss. His tongue slips into my mouth, dancing with mine as I reach for him.

This stupid fucking swing is in the way, so I break the kiss, slink through the tire, and stand up straight.

Miles is grinning at me but doesn't waste any time before he kisses me again. This time, his hands slide to my hips as he backs me up to the tree. He leans his body against mine, his erection pressing into me, and I let out a gasp against his mouth.

This is happening. This is really happening.

Miles Asher is kissing me, and I don't want him to stop.

But of course, he chooses that exact moment to do just that.

He steps back in a rush, his fingers touching his lips as he studies me.

I'm breathing hard as I watch him back.

He smirks.

"Come on," he says and takes another step back. "Let me walk you to your door."

I nod, unsure what I'm supposed to say.

When we get to my apartment, I find myself praying that he kisses me again, but he doesn't.

Instead, he grabs the handle and slides the door open for me.

"Go inside before I kiss you again," he says.

I turn to tell him he should kiss me, maybe even come inside, but he holds a finger to my mouth.

"Go. Inside. Now. *Please.*"

I smile against his finger.

"Only because you said please," I say, finally finding my words. I slip through the doorway, close it, and head down the hallway to my room, where I look back. He's still standing there, only now he's got a hand flat against the side of the apartment and his head is down as if he's debating changing his mind.

That kiss just changed everything between us.

We both know it even though we have no idea what it means, but whether it's tonight or another night, I know for certain it won't stop here.

So why stop now?

To save him the trouble of having to make another choice right now that he will clearly be conflicted over later, I return to the door.

He looks up, relief in his eyes as I bite my bottom lip.

I slide the door open, and he rushes in like a man deprived.

His lips are on mine as he closes the door behind him. I hear the lock.

"Are we sure we want to do this?" I ask, breathless.

He sighs, then runs a hand through his hair as he steps back. "You're right; it's not our thing."

"Right. We argue. That's our thing."

"And fake date."

"Right."

We just stand here, nodding like a couple of bobbleheads.

He's not leaving, and I don't really want him to leave, so …

"How much did you drink?"

"Two beers. I'm fully aware of what's going on here right now. What about you?"

"Same to all of the above." I bite my lip, and that must be his undoing. He rushes me, his lips claiming mine once more.

"This doesn't change anything," I say, letting him walk me backward to the bedroom.

"It's just one night," he adds.

"One night, that's it."

"We give in to this attraction and call it good, finish our agreement, and part ways."

"Deal."

"Deal."

The terms are settled as soon as we reach my room.

Miles reaches down to the hem of my shirt and rips it over my head.

"Fuck," he growls, his eyes locking on my lace bra. "I've thought about the day I'd get to see these, but hell, the lace that's letting your pink nipples play peekaboo is even better than I dreamed."

"So, take it off and see them bare," I say before I can change my mind.

I want him to touch me. I want him to own me. Whatever he wants to give me right now, I'm going to take it.

"Fuck," he groans again. "I'm so hard for you that if you keep saying things like that, I'm going to come in my jeans, and I don't want to do that. Not until I get between your legs and taste how sweet you are."

Oh, lord. I've never been with a man who talks like this.

"Tell me what to do," I whisper, and he pauses.

"You want me to boss you around?"

"In bed, yes," I smirk. "Please."

His eyes close, and the noise that comes from the back of his throat is as much a turn-on as the way he's holding my hips.

Like there's nothing that could make him let go.

In an instant, those hands slide down my legs, grip the back of my thighs, and lift me.

I squeak as I wrap my hands around his neck to hold on.

He turns and presses me to the wall, his hips thrusting forward as his hands busy themselves unclipping and removing my bra. Then his mouth sucks on my right nipple, hard.

"Oh, god," I breathe and claw at the back of his head to find some kind of relief.

He moves to the other breast, and it only makes me scratch at him more.

When he's had enough of me like this, he lowers me to the bed. I expect him to move me to the middle or crawl over me, which is what I want. I so badly want to feel him against me. I want to know how much I turn him on. Is it as much as he does me? I need to know.

Instead, he drops to his knees, tugging my legs until my ass sits at the edge of the bed.

"Lift your hips," he commands, and I obey.

He peels my clothes from my body until I'm bare in front of him.

He spreads my legs wide and then hums.

"You look so pretty soaking wet for me. Did I do that to you?" he asks and then blows on me.

It sends a shiver through my body, and I swear I could come without him touching me. Just knowing he's looking at me and talking to me this way … fuck. It's so hot.

"Answer me," he says, removing his hands from their task of holding me open to him.

"Yes!" I shout, desperate for him to touch me again.

His hands return and slowly, on each inner thigh, slide closer and closer to where I want his mouth.

Finally, he puts me out of my misery. That first lick sends my hips shooting off the bed.

He chuckles, actually chuckles, as one arm comes up to rest over my hip bones, driving me back to the bed.

I can't focus on anything, and I swear my vision goes black as his tongue works me over. Up and down, flicking faster and faster.

"Holy shit, I'm close," I breathe. "So, so close."

As soon as the words are out of my mouth, a finger joins his mouth, and I sit up on the bed as my orgasm shoots through my body.

"Yes, yes, yes," I scream as every inch of my body buzzes with life. My hands instantly grip my breast, and I squeeze, letting this pleasure take its time.

I'm still catching my breath when my gaze connects with Miles's. The look on his face is new for me. His eyes are heated, and his jaw is tight as if he's clenching his teeth together.

"Watching you touch yourself as you came was the hottest thing I've ever seen."

I let out a nervous laugh and cover my eyes with my hands.

"I don't think I've ever come that hard," I admit.

"Good."

He stands up, and that's when I see that his hand is gripping his cock, moving slowly up and down in a twisting motion. I must have been on such a high that I didn't even notice him pushing his jeans and briefs to the floor.

Shit, he's huge.

Long.

Thick.

Smooth.

And the bulging veins.

Why is that so hot to me right now?

"How about instead of sucking that bottom lip into your mouth, you—"

I don't give him a chance to finish. I slide off the bed and fall to my knees in front of him. I think I want this more than he does.

The moan that he lets out the moment my lips touch his head gives me the fire I need to give it my all.

He didn't hold back with me, and I'm not going to do it with him.

One hand wraps around the base of his cock while the other gently cups his balls. I read this in a romance book once and always wondered if it was really as effective as they wrote it to be. No harm in trying new things, right?

"Fuck, fuck, holy fuck," Miles says and then blows out a breath. His fingers lace through my hair, but they don't tug. "Wow. I … you …"

His lack of words makes me pump faster and suck harder.

"Dear god, I'm going to come in less than a minute from your perfect fucking mouth, Quinn. Don't stop. Whatever you do, please. Don't. Stop."

And I don't.

"I'm there. I'm there," he says and attempts to pull back. I grip his butt and hold him in place, swallowing every last drop.

"Fuuuuuuck."

His hips slowly still, and I pull my mouth off him.

His dark gaze is pointed down at me.

"I stand corrected. The sight of you on your knees with my cum glistening off your lips is my new favorite sight."

I lick my lips, and he groans, yanking me up.

"Jesus, Quinn. If you were trying to make a point that you're better at oral than me, you win."

"Good." I smirk and then turn to find my clothes. I wasn't aiming for that, but a little friendly competition never hurt anyone. Especially when it comes to Miles.

I step into my panties and grab a shirt from one of the dresser drawers. Miles watches me the entire time.

I don't say anything and neither does he, but he does finally pull up his boxers and jeans.

Then he rubs the back of his neck as if he isn't sure what to do next.

To save him the pain of thinking of what to say, I beat him to it.

"So, see you in the morning, boss."

The expression on his face morphs from unsure to cocky.

"Yeah," he says slowly with a small growl and takes a step toward me. He cups my chin and presses his lips to mine, hard with dominance. "Just once isn't going to be enough for me."

And he turns and walks out of the room.

As soon as I hear the sliding door close, I cover my face with my hands and fall back onto my bed.

Oh. My. God.

What have we done?

CHAPTER FIFTEEN

MILES

At six o'clock on the dot the next morning, I pound my fist against Luca's front door.

"Luca! Open the door."

Sleep didn't come easy last night. Anytime I closed my eyes, the vision of Quinn on her knees or on the bed spread wide consumed me. I even tried to start my day at four thirty, but I got nothing done. I can't stop thinking about last night.

I fucked up. I fucked up bad.

This is why people should never give in to lust or temptation of any kind.

It's so hard to stop when it's right there in front of you. All pink and wet and—

"Luca, open the goddamn door!"

I hear the click and practically push the door open as I rush inside.

"Jesus, some of us do sleep in the morning. We can't all be workaholics like you."

"We need to talk." I head straight for his kitchen and start a pot of coffee as if it were my own house.

I need a big fucking cup today.

Shit.

I'm a cool guy. I have my shit together, but right now I'm about to lose it.

"O-kay, what's wrong with you?"

"Oh, what's wrong with me? So, so many things." I drop into a seat at his kitchen table and cradle my face in my hands. "Where do I start?"

"There's a whole story? Hell yes." Luca all but claps as he sits across from me with a smile, waiting for me to go on.

I take a deep breath, ready for him to interrupt me after each sentence.

"So, you know my thing with Cherry, right?"

"Yep."

"You know I wanted to avoid her."

"Yep."

"Well, turns out Quinn wanted to avoid some guy, too."

"Who?"

"Doesn't matter."

"It matters to me."

"Still doesn't matter. Anyway, she told her friends, who I don't think she should call that, that she was dating me."

"What? She just made it up when she saw them?"

I shake my head.

"No, she told them last summer."

"You've been dating since last summer."

"No. Pay attention."

"I'm trying."

"She told her … people that she was dating me so that they'd stop trying to set her up with this guy. Fast forward to this summer and those people show up here to get married at the lodge, so Quinn came to me with a plan that both validates her story and helps me keep Cherry away."

"And that was …"

"To fake date. We are fake dating."

"I fucking knew it!" He stands so fast his chair flips onto its back. "There was no way she fell for your grumpy ass that fast. Not to mention, you're always a dick to her."

Was it that fucking obvious to the entire town?

"Anyway," I go on, "the fake dating thing has been working out and Quinn even devised a plan to set Cherry up with the guy she's avoiding."

"Whoa, whoa, so you—"

"But the reason I'm here is because we kissed last night."

His jaw drops.

"And there may have been more than kissing."

His eyes widen.

"We may have taken clothes off."

He slaps his forehead.

"And I want to do it again."

His hands cover his ears.

All in all, this is a very calm Luca response. He's taking it pretty well.

He opens his mouth and then closes it, pacing the kitchen.

"So, are you still fake dating?'

"Yep."

"But not fake fooling around?"

"Is that a thing?"

"I don't know, Miles. You tell me. I didn't think fake dating was a real thing until just now. That's movie shit. Not real life."

"That's what I told her."

"And yet here you are." He puts his hands on his hips and shakes his head at me. "Wow. And we thought I was the one to make rash choices."

"I came here for help, not for you to point out my current flaws."

He grins. "This isn't a flaw. In fact, I think it's great."

"What? How? I just screwed everything up between us."

He leans against the counter and nods toward the coffeepot. "How so?"

As I make myself a cup I say, "Because we were supposed to fake date and then break up, it was an easy plan. Fooling around and oral sex was not part of the plan."

"Whoa, spare me the details."

"I just think you need to know details to see the full depth of this fuck-up."

"You didn't fuck up, but," he says and then stops, the biggest smile on his face forming. "I do love the dramatics right now. Is this how you feel when I talk to you?"

"Luca, I need you to be serious."

"I am. I don't think you fucked up, Miles. You've had a crush on her since the first day you saw her. I'd say this whole thing is overdue. You just had to fake date to get there."

I groan. "I don't think you get it."

"No, I don't think you do. An opportunity was given to you, and you need to open your eyes to figure out what it is and take it before it's gone. Now you have two choices: see where this thing goes with Quinn or call the entire thing off. I think we both know which path you're going to take."

I hear him loud and clear.

Yeah, I do know. But I'm not so sure it's as easy as he thinks.

———

BACK AT THE SHOP, I get straight to work. I don't know that my brother helped me all that much, but knowing he knows what's going on is a weight off my shoulders.

I push back on my roller cart and pop out from under the

Mustang I'm working on. I glance at the clock; Quinn should be coming to work soon.

I've been here almost an hour now.

I've got a lot done, so maybe venting to Luca did help.

Maybe Quinn will want to go for an actual hike today. Just the two of us. I can make time for her, and we can decide where to go from here.

Together. Yeah, that sounds smart.

I inhale and stare at the wall for a moment. I can run a business, but when it comes to Quinn Banks, I have no idea what I'm doing.

As soon as I turn around, I spot Marcus Pepperton walking up the driveway. His eyes are set on me.

I grab my rag from my back pocket and wipe my hands.

"Mr. Asher," he says with a booming voice. "Good to see you."

"It's good to see you as well, Mr. Perpperton. You're out and about early."

I offer to shake his hand, but he looks at it and then shakes his head. "Maybe next time on that handshake."

"Yeah, of course. What can I do for you?"

"I purchased a new car, and I need some work done on it. I was wondering if you could get me in next month. I'll have it shipped and delivered as soon as you can get me in."

I open my mouth to tell him yes, but Quinn has worked really hard to create a balanced schedule for me, and I don't want to insult her by just agreeing.

"Let's go check my schedule. It's been a busy year, but I think we can figure something out."

"Oh, wow," Marcus says. "This looks like a whole new place."

"Yeah, Quinn has done a lot of work since she started. She's been a godsend."

I sit at the computer and pull up the scheduling program she showed me the other day, but it still looks foreign.

I'm about to tell him that I'll have Quinn call, when she walks in with a couple of coffees and a pastry box from B's.

"I went to grab us breakfast," she says quickly but stops short when she sees Cherry's father. I know she knows who he is. It's pretty obvious.

"You must be Quinn," he says and offers her his hand.

She sets the box and drinks down and shakes it. "I am."

"I've heard a lot about you," he says. He doesn't say it in a bad way, but it's clear he's talked to his daughter about us.

"Oh." She laughs nervously. "All good things, I hope?"

He hmmms.

"I wasn't aware that Miles was dating anyone, but I'll admit, once I heard the news, I did a little checking up and found your travel page. Some of your partnerships are with companies I prefer as well. It's very impressive."

"Oh, thank you." Quinn beams. "It's been quite the life."

"And now your next adventure is to stay here in Lovers."

Her smile doesn't falter even one single bit as she turns to look at me.

"Yep."

It's brief, but I can see a spark in her eyes that says she isn't enjoying this conversation right now, and to be frank, neither am I. It's one thing for me to feel threatened by this man, but Quinn deserves a hell of a lot better than that.

I clear my throat. "We're looking at availability for next month for a new project."

"How big is it?" Quinn asks and waves her hands for me to get out of the chair.

"Big. The car currently doesn't run," Marcus answers.

"I don't think there is availability next month or in August, but September has room for one more."

"I like to hear that business is good for you, Miles. I hope it stays that way. Go ahead and put me down, for now."

"Great." Quinn smiles as she keeps her attention on the computer. "Can I help with anything else?"

I shake my head.

"That's all for me." Marcus turns for the door. "See you two around."

"Thank you," I say.

I poke my head out of the office and watch him walk out of the shop, back toward town.

When I turn around, Quinn is grabbing something from the printer.

"I hope you didn't forget that you have interviews today. Your first one should be here in thirty minutes." She nods to the coffee and food on the corner of the desk. "Grab yours."

I do as she says and lean on the desk.

"Are you okay?"

She nods.

"Quinn."

"I'm fine."

I study her for a moment.

I'd been counting down the minutes, wondering how it would be when she walked in. Would she smile? Would she walk up and kiss me? Would she be shy? Would she regret last night?

None of those thoughts included the wrinkle between her eyes laced with worry.

I set my coffee down and squat next to the desk so that I'm at eye level with her. "Are we good?" I cup her face and brush my thumb against her cheek.

She nods. "Yes."

And then she leans away from my touch.

"I'll need details on the Mr. Pepperton job so I can mark off the appropriate amount of time on your schedule."

I stand slowly and nod.

"Of course."

She does a perfect job of looking like she's busy, a clear sign for me to leave.

I don't want to push her, so I give her the space she needs and get back to work.

I don't know Marcus well enough to know if his words were a threat.

I like to hear that business is good for you, Miles. I hope it stays that way.

I hope it does, too and there is only one way to make that happen.

Find a way to take any power that family holds over my business away from them.

The first step is obvious. No matter how much things with Quinn have changed in the last twelve hours, adding more to the situation we are already in isn't smart.

It might not be just my dreams that get crushed in the end anymore, but Quinn's, too.

CHAPTER SIXTEEN

QUINN

I've seen some of the most beautiful landscapes that could make you smile so big your face hurts, but nothing, and I mean nothing, compared to the smile on my face when I woke up this morning.

Last night was amazing.

Yes, I had this fantasy of walking into the shop, Miles would see me and grin, then walk right up to me and kiss me. Maybe even prop me up on the hood of one of his cars and pick up where we left off.

Gah. I hate how far I let that daydream get.

Especially now.

I feel like such a fool.

I woke up and rushed to the bakery for coffee and muffins. We have a full day of interviews, and I thought, if I'm lucky, we'd spend another night on his porch with just the two of us. After the hood moment, of course.

I was so eager to see him. I had confidence that he would be just as happy to see me when I walked in. I mean, you don't have the connection we do and not do more with it, right?

No way.

But none of that happened.

I take a breath and stare at the applicant waiting for Miles to wash up. Miles had asked him to show him how he'd remove the … oh, I don't remember. I know nothing about cars, but I know that the oil that sprayed, causing Miles to clean it up a few minutes ago, isn't right.

The kid has no idea how quickly a person's life can change. He could have had a new job today, but one wrong move and now his chances are gone.

"That's all I have. Thank you," Miles says.

The kid nods. "Yeah, cool. See you later."

And he's gone.

Miles shoves his chair back and heads for the shop door as if the room were on fire.

He's been like this since the moment Cherry's dad left.

Short. Distant. Won't look me in the eyes.

The whole thing made me uncomfortable, too, especially when he mentioned that he looked me up, but I'm not going to let it ruin my entire day. Miles's behavior though, that might ruin it.

I don't know what happens next for us, but if he keeps this up, the only place I see us going is right back to where we were before our deal.

"We have two more interviews today. What is going on?" I ask when he tries to walk out of the office without talking to me.

"Nothing."

"Miles."

"It's nothing, Quinn. Forget it."

"No, I will not forget it. You don't get to do the things we did last night and then pretend like it never happened the next day. It's unacceptable."

Refusing to look at me, he rubs the back of his neck.

"It wasn't anything special."

Oh, hell no.

He's lying.

"Was it Mr. Pepperton?"

"Drop it, Quinn."

"No. Talk to me."

He spins quickly and steps toward me so fast that I instinctively step back.

"Like you talked to me earlier? You said you were fine, and I didn't push it. Why are you pushing it now?"

"Because," I start and let myself think over my words for a moment. "Because I wasn't fine, and I should have told you."

"Yeah, you should have, but since then, I've had time to think about us, and it's not a smart idea."

"What?" I ask as he walks out of the room. "What does that mean?"

"I just think it's better if we keep this exactly as we planned it. If we do anything more, it'll complicate things."

I open my mouth to argue that he should have thought about that before last night, but I don't want to be that girl.

Things … happen. People get caught up in the moment more often than we realize. Emotions run high and lust takes over.

Plus, he's right. It could complicate things.

Ending whatever that was now is for the best.

I give him one firm nod and smile.

"Yeah, we should—"

"Uncle Miles!" A small voice fills the garage, and a tiny body whips between us, crashing into Miles's legs, almost taking him down.

The pained expression he wore seconds ago swiftly morphs into pure joy.

"Maximus, my man!" Miles says back, scooping the kid up and giving him a hug that triggers the boy's deep gut laugh.

"Careful, he just ate his weight in snickerdoodle cookies from B's."

A woman with long dark hair and big brown doe eyes approaches us. Miles's dad is right behind her, which means this must be Ruby.

"Hey, sis," Miles says, still holding her son as he gives her a side hug. "Dad, it's nice to see you today."

"You too," he says. "Quinn, you look lovely today." His dad hugs me and then Ruby claps.

"Oh my gosh, you're Quinn?"

I nod.

Now it's her turn to wrap me in her arms.

"Sadie has told me so much about you, and I am absolutely loving this for my brother."

Miles just rolls his eyes. "What are you doing here?" he quickly changes the topic.

His dad clears his throat. "We actually need a favor."

"Yeah, sure, anything," Miles says.

This a family thing. I give a small wave and turn for the office.

"Oh, this involves you, Quinn, so can you hang on just a moment before you get back to work?"

Me? How could this involve me?

"Of course."

"I'm moving back," Ruby says and smiles. "For good."

"Seriously?" Miles beams. "Colter finally caved?"

Ruby keeps a smile on her face, but their dad speaks up. "Max, let's go check out Miles's new house, should we?"

"Did he put in a tire swing?"

"There's a good chance."

Max races out the back, his grandfather right behind him.

Miles crosses his arms. "What happened? Did he cheat on you?"

Ruby shakes her head.

"No, it wasn't anything like that. We…" She fidgets with her hands as she looks away. "We broke up a few months ago."

"What? A few months ago? And you didn't tell us?"

"Should I go?" I ask quickly.

Ruby shakes her head.

"It's a long story, Miles. But everything is fine. Colter is even happy that I'm coming back, and Max will grow up here."

"Yeah, okay. Sure," Mile says. The sarcasm in his voice is lethal.

"It's the truth, but the thing is, I'm moving in with Dad because the school is just down the block. But the last thing I need is him hovering over me right now. I need to be the best mom I can be right now to Max."

"Maybe you need Dad to hover."

God, he sounds like my brother.

"What I need is for him to move into the apartment you built him."

Ah. The part where I come in.

Miles shakes his head. "Quinn is living there. I'm not kicking her out. She'd be go—" He cuts himself off. "I'm not kicking her out."

"I know," Ruby says softly, "but I was hoping that since she's been staying with you anyway, maybe she could just keep doing that."

She wants me to move in with Miles? I don't need a mirror to know that my eyes are wide as saucers right now.

He just said he wants space, and I've been in his house enough times to know that none of his spare rooms are furnished. Where would I sleep?

On the couch?

"I … we …" Miles starts. His face is clear right now that he has no idea how to reply to this request.

"We would love to help," I say quickly before he starts to sweat.

I step forward and touch his arm so that he knows I'm aware of what this means right now. The hole we are digging just keeps getting deeper.

"When do you need me to move my things?"

"Is today too soon?" she asks with nervous laughter.

I shake my head. "Today is perfect. I even think I'll have time to clean for you."

"You don't need to do that."

"I insist," I tell her and squeeze Miles's arm a little harder. Is he zoning out right now? What's his deal?

He looks up quickly. "Yes, yes, Quinn will move in with me, and Dad can be in the apartment, right next door to us, where we will be living and where he can see us anytime he wants."

Ruby laughs at her brother's awkwardness, while I try not to cringe.

So that's where his mind is.

Freaking out. Got it.

"It's his first time living with a girl who isn't me." Ruby looks at me. "Give him some slack for being dumb right now."

At that she slugs his shoulder and walks right by him for the back door.

"It was great meeting you, Quinn!" she shouts over her shoulder as she disappears.

I just stand there next to Miles, who has gone mute.

Obviously, the last thing he wants is for me to move in, and I get it.

"I can go back to my brother's," I tell him. "Or my grand-mother's."

His gaze snaps to mine. "And tell them what? That we broke up?"

"Or that we are two mature adults who know this is still new and don't want to rush it."

He shakes his head. "It'll still lead to questions, and this is a small town."

"I've noticed."

"You'll move in with me."

"Miles, I—"

"You're moving in, Quinn. I already told them it was fine. It'll look weird if we change that now."

I cross my arms and glare at him. "You seem to be calling a lot of shots lately. I don't remember making you the boss of this arrangement."

"That you started."

"Oh my god. Are we really going back to this? Back to never getting along because you don't want to get close to me?"

He sighs and rubs a hand over his face.

"No. We aren't."

"Then what are we doing?"

"We are getting through the rest of this summer as a fake couple, just like we planned. That's it."

Then he walks out the back to join his family, leaving me alone in the shop.

My chest aches at the emotional roller coaster this day has already put me through.

I was fine when I didn't know Miles and he didn't care for me.

But now that I know him better, him not caring for me … that hurts.

———

"I'M SO sorry to kick you out so soon," Mr. Asher says from the chair in the apartment's living room.

I was just grabbing my last suitcase when he showed up.

"It's not a problem," I tell him and look around to make sure I didn't miss anything.

"Well, it was last-minute, and I told Ruby that we needed to wait, but she had other plans."

"It's really fine."

It really sucks, but that's for me to worry about and not him.

The sliding door opens and Miles steps through. His eyes find me immediately, and I swear he starts to smile but then quickly changes his mind.

"All settled, Dad?" he asks, grabbing my last suitcase. He'd been over at his house when I bought my first bag over. I left my second bag on his porch so that I didn't have to face him again so soon.

He must have seen it and made his way over to help.

"I can get it. It's the last one."

"It's okay."

"I can get it," I say again in the nicest *fuck off* way I can in front of his father.

"But you shouldn't have to." Miles looks me square in the eye.

"That's how I raised them, despite the execution of his gesture." Mr. Asher leans back and glares at his son. "Let's use a little more kindness and a little less growl next time, yeah?"

I pinch my lips together to hold in my laugh, but it still bubbles in my chest. Miles catches the moment I cough and look away.

"I'll meet you at the house," I say quickly and then wave to Mr. Asher. "Good night."

"Good night, Quinn."

I close the sliding door behind me and glance over my scheduler to see Miles nodding as Mr. Asher talks.

Is he giving him advice? Is he scolding him for his tone just now?

I was ready to tell Miles off on my own. Once we are out of his father's earshot, of course.

I sigh as I make my way inside Miles's home.

This house is a dream, and under any other circumstance, I'd enjoy that I'm moving in, but right now, I'm just flustered.

After his family left earlier, I went back to the office to finish as much work as I could and rescheduled the remaining interviews. Then I went back to get packed and clean the apartment.

Why did Ruby need her dad to move out so suddenly? If my parents had a permanent home, I wouldn't mind having to live with them, so why didn't she want to live with their dad? I'm sure there is more to the story, and it's not my place to ask.

Maybe I could have asked Miles if he and I actually spoke once they left, but we didn't. We haven't talked about this at all other than agreeing that I would do it.

I put my hands on my hips and wander down the hallway on the main floor. There is a spare room on the first door to the right. I push the door open to reveal an empty space.

I shake my head.

"What kind of person doesn't furnish their spare rooms?" I wonder aloud to myself.

"The kind whose only visitors are people who already live in this town and who did furnish it but then built his father an apartment and moved the furniture there."

Miles. I turn to face him.

"I didn't mean it like that."

"You did."

Jesus, we could go rounds with any topic, couldn't we?

I fold my arms in front of my chest. "I'm not sleeping on the floor or the couch."

He rolls his eyes as if that's old news.

"You can sleep in my room."

"I'm not sleeping in there with you."

Ignoring me, he turns for the stairs. "I'll go put fresh sheets on the bed."

"So, what now? I repulse you again?"

"What?" He stops on the first step.

"I hate you. I like you. Let's be friends. Just kidding, let's kiss, let's take your clothes off. No, wait, bad idea. Let's hate each other again. I can't keep up with you," I snap and move for the kitchen.

"Is that your impression of me?" Miles follows close behind me.

I spin around, causing him to step back.

"Yes. That's exactly you."

"Then you must be blind, Quinn."

"Ha. I'm not blind."

"Clearly, you are." He moves for the stairs again.

"Okay, prove me wrong. How is it?"

"Why am I the bad guy?"

"Um, because I was happy to continue what happened last night and you're the one who decided it was a mistake."

"I never said that."

"What you said earlier is pretty much the same thing."

He shakes his head.

"It's not."

"Oh. My. God." With my hands at the side of my head, I make an explosion gesture. "I can't keep up. Just say what you're thinking. A full explanation would be nice."

"I … will put clean sheets on the bed for you."

I don't know why that statement sets me off even more, but it does.

I march up the steps right behind him.

"I can do it myself. Just show me where the sheets are."

"I'm going to do it."

"No, I will."

"Quinn, stop."

"No, you stop. If you want things how they always have been, then stop doing nice things for me."

"I can't!"

"Why not?"

"Because I don't want things to go back to how they were!"

He's breathing heavily now as he paces behind the bed twice, then sits on the edge.

"Do you really believe that after last night, I don't want you? Hell, Quinn, I'm trying to push you away to help you. Don't make this any harder than it needs to be."

He looks away from me as if it actually hurts him to see me standing in front of him. I take a tentative step toward him, reaching out to cup his cheek and make him look at me.

"Help me how?"

His eyes connect with mine, and his throat bobs as he swallows the lump in his throat. He reaches for my legs, his fingers caressing the back of my thighs for one quick stroke each before he stands quickly. He squeezes my hand twice before he drops it.

"Just trust me," he says with a little more control and then opens his closet door to pull out some sheets.

I start to take the ones off his bed. "Right now, you're the only one not making this easy, by not telling me the full story."

His gaze drifts to mine briefly before he sits on the bed again.

"If Mr. Pepperton can take my career away, he can take yours, too."

Every word is spoken with defeat, and I didn't realize how much that would affect me.

I move in front of him again to make sure he hears me loud and clear.

"Whatever Mr. Pepperton does is not on you. His choices will never be your fault."

"They might be. If we hadn't decided to do this whole fake dating thing, you wouldn't even be on his radar, Quinn. Now you're at the top of the list with me."

"Do you know this for a fact?"

"No, but his comments this morning didn't change my mind."

I let out a big sigh.

"We never should have started this stupid idea."

He's right. It's not the first time we've come to this conclusion, but it's the first time we might actually follow through on a breakup plan.

"Well, I guess that means we have only one option."

"What's that?"

"We break up before the summer is over."

He shakes his head.

"I don't think it's that easy. For one, Cherry could still try to get to me and Danny to you. That guy is a tool, and it fucking bothers me that he thinks he stands a chance. If we do that, this whole thing will have been for nothing."

I let a smile touch my lips.

"Don't worry, Miles. I won't be running to Danny."

"Still doesn't change the fact that they might try."

"It would be a real dick move to hit on someone mending a broken heart, even if it's not real."

I take a breath and step back. Miles watches my every move, his eyes taking me in from my bare legs all the way until he reaches my eyes.

I know I said it wouldn't be real, but for some reason, this discussion makes it feel the complete opposite.

"How will we do it?" he finally asks.

I say the first thought that comes to mind.

"I think we should do it at the Fourth of July festival in just over two weeks. It'll be public, and we know everyone will be there for the big fireworks show."

He nods. Then he goes back to making the bed.

Miles doesn't speak again while we finish with the sheets, which is just another reminder that this is it.

My first fake relationship has run its course.

And a part of me is wishing that it isn't fake and that it isn't going to end so soon.

CHAPTER SEVENTEEN

MILES

My back hurts.

Fuck.

Being in your thirties isn't old, but that couch is ready to put up a damn good argument.

I groan and roll off the sofa, rubbing my back and arching backward, stretching in a way that I don't think the body should ever be stretched. Well, not mine anyway.

I hear two pops before I let out a deep breath.

It's only for a couple of weeks.

As soon as we get through the next fourteen days, it's breakup time and back to normal life we go.

I know I'm a workaholic and I can be pretty strict in my free time, but the small pieces of fake dating we did do in public were a nice break. It was a fresh reminder that there is more to life than work. There is more to life than pretending to date someone, too, but baby steps here.

I wander into the kitchen to start some coffee, and my fake girlfriend herself strolls in. Her hair is in a messy bun on top of her head, she's wearing a red pajama set with white slippers, and the sleepy dazed look in her eyes gives her this whole innocent look.

I'll admit this, too: seeing Quinn the moment she wakes up is not the worst thing. In fact, I can't remember the last time I smiled this much over a woman in my kitchen, if ever.

It might have something to do with the fact that Quinn isn't expecting anything from me right now. I think we can agree that the morning after sex can be unpredictable, but since that's not the case with us, I can do whatever I want with no consequences. Funny thing is, though, I want to do something for Quinn, and I wish this were the morning after sex.

"I'm making coffee and was about to cook some bacon and eggs. Do you want some?"

"Mmm, that sounds delicious. Yes, please."

She moves for the fridge, grabs the creamer, and stands next to the coffeepot. I maneuver around her to reach the fridge, pulling out what I need and returning to her other side.

"Sleep okay?" I ask.

"Yep. You?"

I let out a little laugh. "Not even a little."

"Oh." The sleepy expression turns to a frown. "We should switch."

"Hell no," I say quickly. "Now that I know how bad the couch sucks, I'd never let you sleep on it."

She smirks.

"That's oddly kind of you."

To that I smile.

"I think we can agree that whatever is going on between us is … well, just expect the unexpected."

"Oh, you've never been more right."

The coffeepot stops, so Quinn pours a cup for herself and one for me.

She doesn't move as she takes her first sip.

The moan that escapes her makes me freeze.

It's not a sex moan, and it's not a this *feels great* moan. It's a *this coffee is yummy* groan of appreciation, and yet I instantly grow hard in my shorts.

I close my eyes and take a deep breath as I stir the eggs.

Last night when we were making my bed, I wanted to kiss her. I didn't want our night to end the way it did, but fuck, I'd just told her why we couldn't do anything more than what's going on now, and then we agreed to break up. Kissing her would have been … it would have been me doing exactly what she said. Being someone who basically gives her whiplash.

She's not wrong.

I'm just having a hard time controlling the way I'm feeling.

I want her, but she isn't staying, and everything is getting complicated.

How can I get what I want and then just watch her leave when the summer is over?

Simple.

I dig deep. Really fucking deep and use self-control.

"Why don't you sleep in your room with me tonight?"

"No."

Her sigh can probably be heard all the way over at my dad's apartment.

"If the couch sucks, you shouldn't sleep on it, and your bed is big enough for the two of us."

I blow out another breath.

"No. The couch will be fine for a couple of weeks. I don't want to intrude on your space."

"Oh, please. I'm the one who took over your room."

She steps closer to me to look at the bacon cooking in the pan, her chest brushing up against me.

"Shit, sorry." She steps back.

"It's fine," I grumble, even though now all I can think about is that she's not wearing a bra.

"Breakfast looks good. Thanks for cooking."

She pulls two plates from my cupboard and sets them by the pan.

"I'll shower and get ready after we eat."

And then it happens again: her body brushes up against me.

I don't know if it was an accident or intentional, but the self-control I'm practicing is growing very thin.

I adjust my stance to hide my erection as I dish our plates and set them on the table.

I swear to god, if she moans while eating, I will shove every fucking thing off this table and eat her for breakfast instead of the meal I cooked.

If she wants to moan because of something I've done, it won't be from my goddamn cooking.

Jesus, I'm in a mood this morning.

The ding of my phone distracts me from any more thoughts of Quinn on my kitchen table. The drop-down on my screen is a notification from the pet place I emailed about their golden retriever puppies. I open it quickly, read the email, and then hold it up for Quinn.

"Look, they approved me."

"Who?" she asks as she takes the phone. "Oh my god! You're getting a dog!"

I grin and take my phone back, reading the remainder of the email.

"Wow. I can go as early as today to pick one out."

"Let's do it."

I set the phone down, then take a quick bite. "Can't. I have to work."

Quinn rolls her eyes.

"And last I checked, you're the boss, so you can play hooky if you want."

"That's no way to run a business."

"Yeah, if you do it every day, but once in the entire time you've owned that shop isn't going to hurt anything."

"How do you know I've never played hooky before?"

"Oh, please, Miles. I don't have to live here to know that you love your work more than anything else in this world."

Now it's my turn to roll my eyes.

A couple of days ago, she would have been right, but I don't think right now is the time to remind her of my new favorite things.

"I think we need to go get you this dog today."

I take one more bite, letting her words sink in.

I mean, it would be a good reason to skip out on work. I wouldn't mind having a dog right now. Something to keep me busy.

"What's on my schedule today?"

"All restoration work. No appointments."

It's as if it were meant to be.

I nod before I can change my mind.

"All right, let's do it."

"Yay! Road trip," she cheers and then shoves the last of her eggs into her mouth. She sets her dish in the sink and takes off up the stairs, leaving me at the table with nothing but a smile on my face.

Why is it that every day I'm with her, she surprises me more and more?

I grab my phone to let the breeders know I'll be there in a few hours.

Then I glance back to the stairs.

I only get a limited number of mornings like this before our arrangement is over.

Why does the thought of that make my chest ache?

———

"How are you supposed to pick just one?" Quinn whispers to me.

The gal who's selling the puppies led us to a pen in her backyard and said there are five puppies left. Two boys and three girls.

My instinct says to pick a boy, but this girl at my feet seems to be smitten with me.

Quinn crouches down to pick her up and hands her to me. Then she grabs another.

"What if you get two?" Her eyes go wide as if it's the best idea in the world.

"No, no, no, I can't handle two puppies."

"But then we would each have one. I've never had a puppy before."

"Really?" I ask, leaning away from the girl in my arms as she licks my face profusely. "Never?"

"I travel too much."

Yeah, I guess I could have figured that out.

I lower myself to sit crisscross, and so does Quinn. The puppies play all around us, and damn, she's right, it's going to be hard to pick just one.

"Why did you start traveling?" I ask, taking any reason to distract myself right now. How do I pick just one of these furballs?

Quinn doesn't respond right away, so I glance up. She's studying me.

"Why are you asking me this now?"

I shrug. I have no idea.

Ever since last night and our agreement to break up, I feel

lighter. Like … I don't know. Like I can get to know her now on my terms and not under some false pretense.

"Let's just say it's something I should have asked you a long time ago."

She smirks. "Well, my parents got me started young. Legally, I had to go where they went, and then after so many years, traveling felt more normal than not traveling. I could attend college online at a lot of places, so that worked out well. I really haven't known anything different since I was a teenager."

I get it. My family knew the small-town life, and that's what they passed down to me. Same for Quinn but with traveling.

I've been judging her for living the life she knows, when that's exactly what I've been doing. The fact she was able to turn something she loves into a paid career is even more impressive. I, too, was able to find a job I love, but it's a lot harder than you think.

"Well, I'm glad some of your family found Lovers."

"Me too." She bites her bottom lip and looks away. "Okay, I have an idea."

"What's that?"

"You choose a name, and the first dog to respond to it is the dog we pick."

"I like it."

I also like the way she says *we*.

"Okay, what's the name?"

"I don't know yet."

"Miles!"

"What? I've had other things on my mind. Plus, I sort of thought I'd know which dog I wanted when I got here and a name would just come to me."

Quinn shakes her head with a smile. "You're something else."

"Yeah." I pick a few strands of grass from the yard, tossing it at her. "So are you."

"At least I have name ideas."

"Let's hear them."

"Buddy."

"Too common."

"Rocky."

"Pass."

"Max."

"Eh."

"Charlie."

"Too human."

"Too human," she repeats with a laugh. "Okay."

"That's it?"

She pinches her lips together and then sighs. "I have one more, but I don't know if I should tell you."

"Why not?"

"Because it's from a movie, and anytime I think of this one scene from the movie, I want to cry, but I just love the name so much."

"Does it have a golden retriever?"

She nods.

"If you say Shadow, I'm stealing it."

"No! What if I get a dog someday? Then what? Our dogs will have the same name."

"Yep. Shadow!" I yell, not giving her any time to argue with me.

The boy pup in her lap yelps and licks her right across the mouth.

Quinn falls back with a laugh.

I think we have a winner.

———

WE PULL BACK into Lovers by mid-afternoon, and instead of driving straight for the shop, I drive down Main Street and park in front of the bakery.

"What are we doing here?"

"I'm grabbing some snacks for later."

"Do they make dog treats?"

"Not for the dog," I laugh. "For me."

I get out before she asks more about it. Today has been oddly relaxing, and the company has far exceeded my expectations.

Brooke is behind the cash register today. Her hands go to her hips instantly. "Miles, hey, where have you been all day?"

"Why? Did I miss something good?"

Shakes her head. "Unless you're referring to Luca blowing a gasket that your shop was closed today, then no."

I chuckle.

"So, where were you?"

"Yeah, where were you?" a voice from behind me asks, and I spin to find Luca himself standing in the doorway.

"If the two of you must know, I went to Wind Valley to get a dog."

"For who?" my brother asks, and I glare at him.

"For myself."

"A dog, really?"

"Yes, really. Why is that so hard to believe?"

"Dogs are a big responsibility."

"Your point?"

"My point is, you work a lot. What's it going to do, sit in your shop with you all day?"

I nod. "Yes."

Luca crosses his arms, but instead of waiting to see what he's going to say next, I give Brooke my order. She rings me up, cashes me out, then hands me my goodies.

Luca is still standing in the same spot.

"Anything else?" I ask.

"You're being weird," he says and points at me. "Where is the wrinkle between your eyes?"

"Seriously?"

"Yes."

"I don't think I'm the one being weird. You are."

As I stride past him, he groans.

"No. Not you, too. No, no, noooo."

I know I should keep walking, but he's my best friend and twin brother and he knows exactly how to make me take the bait.

"What now?"

"You're pulling a Hudson on me."

"I'm not pulling a Hudson. Hell, I don't even know what that means."

"It means, you're being all happy and shit but pretending it's not because you're in love."

I hold my hands up.

"I'm not in love."

He slaps his cheeks.

"You're already in the denial phase. That wasn't one of the options from yesterday morning, Miles."

"I'm not in denial. You're being crazy."

"Oh god, I'm going home. All alone. The only Asher son left. What will I do? Who will I hang out with? Not that we hang out much anymore anyway, but what will—"

"Stop, stop," I cut him off as Brooke laughs behind us. I glance at my watch and then back to him. "Come over in a couple of hours, and we can grill burgers. I'll call Hudson, Dad, and Ruby when I get home."

Luca's bottom lip drops, but no words come out.

I chuckle as I walk out of the bakery, and at that exact moment, I see Quinn taking a selfie with Shadow. Then she kisses his forehead and hugs him.

I'm not in love.

It's impossible to love someone you're not actually dating and have disliked for the last however many years.

It just doesn't happen like that.

It doesn't.

"Hey," Quinn says as she rolls her window down. "We should go get him a bed for the house, my office, and your shop."

Her smile lights up her entire face.

And there's no way I can say no to a smile like that.

CHAPTER EIGHTEEN

QUINN

Puppies are so freaking cute.

But you know what I like best about this particular puppy? It's the way Miles is holding him cradled on his back in one arm while he sips a beer with the other.

He's all man, but Shadow is so tiny that the whole image is screaming, *I know how to be gentle.*

Now, that is tempting.

Which is all kinds of messed up because … because … we had our chance to be a couple and we struggled with it. Now we are breaking up, and if I'm a smart woman, I'll get any and all thoughts of Miles as anything more than what we are out of my head.

It wouldn't work.

We both know it.

We made things complicated, and even though we are trying to fix the mess we made, it's just smart if I don't add fuel to the fire.

Even though just being around him today has been enlightening.

Miles knows how to relax, and it's a good look for him.

Too good.

I can picture myself spending too much time with this version of Miles.

"How's it going over here?" Sadie asks as she sits on the porch swing next to me.

To say I was blown away that Miles was having his family over for dinner was an understatement. We got back to town early, and I was convinced that he'd head to the garage straight away. He'd ditched work—also mind-blowing—to get this puppy, and I could have sworn he was itching to get back to work in the shop, but no, he wanted to go get all the things for Shadow and then plan dinner for his family.

Now, he's laughing with his brothers, Ruby, Max, and his dad over a game of cornhole.

Dinner with his family, games, beers, and his dog. This life looks good on him.

"I'm just admiring this view while I still can," I say honestly. It's nice to have someone who knows the truth.

"The view as in the lake and mountains or my soon-to-be brother-in-law?"

She's got a knowing look in her eyes as she waits for my answer. But I don't say anything. She bumps my shoulder with hers.

"It sneaks up on you, doesn't it?"

"I don't know what you're talking about."

She sighs. "You can deny it all you want, but as someone who knows from personal experience, once you fall for an Asher, that's it. You won't come back from it."

"I didn't fall for Miles," I correct her quickly, but there's a good chance I'm saying this for my benefit and not just hers. If I keep repeating it, maybe my brain can understand why we wouldn't work. The list is long. Friends are all we should be. "In fact, we are breaking up next weekend."

"What?" Sadie says so loudly and with so much shock that the men in the yard stop their conversation to look at us.

Hudson takes a step this way, but Sadie holds her hand up. My eyes connect with Miles's. His gaze narrows as if he's trying to figure me out, so I look away quickly. But I still feel his eyes on me. When I glance once more, I'm not surprised that he's still watching me.

"That does not look like the face of a man who plans to break up next weekend."

I nod and then sip the wine she brought over.

"It just makes sense that we end things now. We've seen Cherry around town with Danny, so we're pretty sure she's distracted. Plus, I'm sure Miles wants his bedroom back, not to mention his life. One that isn't full of lies."

"I don't know," Sadie says with a grin. "The Miles I'm seeing tonight is pretty good. I haven't seen him this laid-back since Hudson and I got together. He's always very grumpy."

"So grumpy," I say with a laugh. "And he gets this little wrinkle between his eyes when he looks at you. Like it actually hurts him to be standing there having a conversation with another person."

"Mmm," Sadie hums. "That might just be when he's talking to you."

I roll my eyes. "Sadie, if Miles and I get any sort of relationship out of this summer, it'll be friendship."

She holds her hands up. "Fine. Fine. I'll drop it, but just know, it's okay if you pick a different path with him."

I toss back the last of my drink, like a woman taking a shot, not a woman who should be sipping wine.

"I'm going to get a refill. Do you want one?"

"Yes, please."

I take her glass and then head inside.

I grab the bottle we'd opened, but it's empty, so I start opening cabinets to see if Miles has more.

The polite thing would be to ask where it's at, but that would mean he'd have to come in here, and that would put us alone in a room, and right now, I don't think that's—"

"Looking for something?"

I startle at the sound of Mile's voice.

Damn. He made it inside anyway.

"Just another bottle of wine. I'm not feeling the beer tonight."

He nods and goes to a cabinet I hadn't reached yet. He grabs a bottle of something red and opens it for me.

"What were you and Sadie talking about?" he asks as he refills both our glasses.

I cross my arms and look down. "I told her we are planning the breaking up."

"You did? What did she say?"

I shake my head. "Nothing."

"Are you lying to me?"

I shake my head again, but this time, it feels like it's in slow motion.

"So, she didn't tell you she thought it was silly because she and Hudson think we aren't faking it anymore?"

I toss my head back with a laugh.

"You told Hudson?"

He shrugs. "I thought it might help to have a backup if needed."

I blow out a breath. "Yeah, Sadie said something along those lines."

I expect him to ask me what I think about their assumptions, but he doesn't.

And I'm glad.

What would I even say?

If I told him I agreed, would we still break up?

See, this is exactly why you do not fake date anyone. It becomes complicated really fast, and now I can't even think straight.

Before I can say anything stupid, I reach for one of the brownies he picked up from B's Bakery earlier.

"Are these your favorite? I noticed you had them last week, too."

He nods.

"You could just bake your own."

"It's not the same."

"Why not?"

He sighs and then leans on the counter. "Grabbing brownies or another treat from B's was a thing my mom and I used to do together. Anytime I accomplished something I'd been wanting; I got a treat."

"And today, you accomplished getting a puppy."

"I did."

I hold the brownie out for him, and he splits it in two.

As he takes a bite, I ask, "And what did you accomplish last week?"

He finishes chewing, swallows, and grabs his beer, heading for the door.

I don't think he's going to answer me, but he stops and looks over his shoulder.

"Those were because I finally found a reason to get to know the mysterious Quinn Banks. The cookies in the cupboard to your left are because I finally kissed you."

And then he walks right out the door, leaving me stunned.

He glances back once with a smile.

Then he winks.

Oh, no.

Oh, no, no, no.

I fell for my fake boyfriend.

———

As soon as everyone left, I tried to clean the kitchen as quickly as I could. Sadie and I drank another bottle between just the two of us, and that alone wasn't smart.

Alcohol mixed with whatever I'm feeling for Miles isn't a good pairing. Well, they're actually a fantastic pair and could be a lot of fun, but I'm trying to be an adult here.

I should be focusing on where I'm headed next on an airplane or at least sending emails so I can start planning. Not letting thoughts of Miles crowd my brain at all times of the day.

Seriously.

How does one even function when they acquire feelings for someone? How long does the fascination last?

"Oh, you already cleaned," Miles says from the doorway to the kitchen.

I'm just closing the dishwasher.

"I still need to wipe the counters down, but yep, almost done."

"I'll finish. I really didn't think you were going to do all of this. I wouldn't have walked my dad back if I knew you were here cleaning alone."

"It's fine. Really."

I reach for the cleaning supplies at the same time as Miles.

Our hands touch and we both jump back as if we burned each other. Then our gazes collide, and we both break out in laughter.

"Why are we like this?" he asks.

"I don't know."

His face turns serious. "I do. I don't know why I even asked. Because I'm trying to convince myself otherwise, I guess."

I take a breath but don't respond.

"Maybe if we just—" he starts.

"Gave in—"

"One more time—"

"Then we can get over this tension—"

"And go back to being us."

I hear him and I'm right there with him, but it doesn't match what he said yesterday. One day can't change that, can it?

"You said you didn't want to complicate things," I say, my head tilting back as he steps closer.

He groans into my ear. "I know."

"I'm starting to think you don't know what complicated means, Miles."

His hand brushes my hip as he backs me up to the kitchen island.

"I'm aware of what it means, Quinn. But when it comes to you, I don't care anymore."

His lips press gently to the spot right under my ear, and I have to take a deep breath. My brain can't put together coherent sentences when he does this. When he's this close. When the smell of him overwhelms me and makes me want things I shouldn't want.

This will indeed complicate things.

We both know it, and yet we can't seem to stop.

Still, I have to at least try, right?

"So, we should stop, right?" I regret the words as soon as they spill from my lips. I don't really want to stop. I can only hope he doesn't want too either.

Miles leans back, a sly grin taking over his lips.

"Is that what you want?"

Our eyes lock, and I inhale.

"No."

"Good."

His hands cup my face, and he crashes his lips to mine. Bliss rushes through my veins once again, warming every inch of my body and causing my heart to race.

The rush of his kiss is nothing I've ever felt before, and now that he's done it a second time, I'm not sure I can ever go back.

He breaks this kiss only to give me more on my jaw, my neck, down to my chest. One of his hands slides over my nipple and pops the top button of my shirt, giving his mouth access to kiss and lick his way down the valley between my breasts. His hands smooth over my shorts and down my butt until his fingers reach the end of the fabric. His hand curls, tugging at my shorts.

"Oh, god," I whimper.

Why does his touch feel like I'm on a high?

It's hard to make connections with people when you aren't sticking around, but this, with Miles—it's different.

Even though we never spent time getting to know one another, I know him, and he knows me. The tension between us was bound to snap, even more so after that night in my room.

Add in the fact we decided to play fake boyfriend and girl-friend and I'd be lying if it weren't in the back of my mind somewhere that this is where we would end up again.

But right here in the kitchen, I can confidently say I didn't imagine this.

Since the buttons on my shirt don't go all the way down, he moves his hands from my hips to my stomach, slipping them under my shirt.

Then he rips it over my head.

"Fuck, that's so much better."

Miles reaches down to grip behind my thighs, picking me up as if I weigh absolutely nothing, and sets me on top of the island. Each hand grips a knee as he kisses me hard.

He spreads my legs and stands between them.

Fuck, that was hot. I like that. I like it a lot.

And yet, I'd like it a whole lot of more if he weren't wearing pants either.

"Lift your butt," he breathes into my ear, and I don't have to think twice. I do as I'm told, and he grins, pulling off my underwear.

"Ohhh, god, are we really doing this again?" I ask. It comes out all breathy and wanting and the hungry look in his eye tells me he knows me all too well.

"If by this you mean I'm about to bury my face between your legs until you come all over my tongue and lose all ability to control yourself, yes, we are doing this."

The thump of my heart picks up with every word that leaves his mouth. I want all of that. Consequences be damned and he knows it.

"Now," he says and sits at one of the island chairs, his face lined up with where my butt sits on the edge. "Put your legs on my shoulders and show me your beautiful pussy. I've missed it and have been waiting to see her again."

I want to argue. I want to tell him that even though I told him I liked to be bossed around, it doesn't always mean he's going to get his way, but right now I don't do any of that. I want my way, and my way says to take the orgasm I know he's about to give me and save the arguing for later.

I do as he's instructed and watch as he takes me in.

His tongue slips from his mouth to lick his lips, and the small gesture makes me moan.

The throaty sound is like a signal to lose all control, because he grips my thighs, jerks me closer, and buries his face between my legs.

"Oh, shit, yes," I call out, dropping from my hands to my

forearms. The movement raises my hips just slightly, but that doesn't stop Miles.

Nope.

He continues to feast as if someone were timing him, sending him racing for the finish line.

"Miles," I cry out when his pace only increases. I balance on one arm so that I can slide my fingers through his hair. My head tilts back with another moan.

"Oh, this feels so good," I say.

"Enjoy it, baby, because once I'm inside of you, nothing is going to feel as hypnotizing as the way my cock is going to stretch and fill you."

His words send a shiver through my body.

I want that, too.

So, so badly.

His mouth is back on me in record time, but this time, he slides a finger in, joining his tongue. Then two, then three.

"Ahh," I say as he fingers and licks me with crazed passion. "It's too much. It's … it's … it's …"

I suck in a breath as the tingle of my orgasm rips through my body.

"Fuck yeah, baby, I can feel you pulsing on my fingers, and I love it."

His face dives back in, his tongue taking over for his hand, and I ride out the wave of pure bliss.

When I finally catch my breath, Miles is standing by the island, shaking out my shorts and handing me my underwear.

"I have to be honest with you, Quinn. I've seen you touch yourself, come on my face, and I've seen you with your lips wrapped around my dick. I just can't decide what I like most."

And then he kisses my lips, biting my bottom one as he pulls back.

I lock my legs around his waist and pull him toward me with my heels so that I can deepen the kiss.

With a hand on each of my hips, he squeezes and then glides them up to my chin. He tilts my head back so that he can lick and press his lips to my neck.

"I need to take you upstairs so that I can see what you look like with my cock inside you. After that, maybe I can decide."

"Yes," I moan. I want that, too.

My pleading response might be enough, but just to be sure, I hollow out my stomach to make room for my hand. I then unbuckle his pants and slide my hands inside his boxers.

He's hard, and when I push his pants down, his erection springs free, begging to be taken care of.

Miles scoots me off the counter, holding me with my legs wrapped tight around him as he moves for the stairs.

"As much as I'd love to fuck you in my kitchen, I'm not letting that be the first place I take you. Nor the second or the third."

His words turn me on all over again. Whatever this man has planned for me, I'm into it.

I grab his erection again and begin to stroke him.

He slams me to the wall at the base of the stairs and kisses me hard. "Someone's impatient."

"It's hard not to be when this is what I have to look forward to."

He groans, my hand never slowing its strokes.

"How am I supposed to go upstairs while you do that? Fuck, it feels good."

I lean forward, biting his ear. "Just think of how reaching the top means you get to lay me on your bed and sink your—ah!" I squeal as he races up the stairs. I'm still in his arms, but he moves as if I weigh nothing.

He's down the hall, in his room, and tossing me onto the bed in seconds.

"Remove the rest of your clothes and open your legs."

God, this man and his orders.

I do as I'm told and watch as his hungry eyes take me in. He loves when I listen, and I love the reward I get when I do.

He pulls his shirt over his head, and I sigh at the sight of him. How did I let this man get by me so many times?

Then he strips his jeans and briefs off, standing in front of me completely naked with his hard-on in his hand.

The first time with someone is usually nerve racking and can make someone a little shy, but with Miles, it's not like that at all.

His eyes roam over my body like I'm a treat he can't wait to sink his teeth into. He smiles at me, and I've never felt safer.

"I'm confident both of us are clean and that neither of us have been with anyone in a while, but we should still use a condom," he says.

His honesty makes me melt inside.

"Okay" is all I say. I feel the same way he does.

He moves to the bedside dresser and pulls out a single gold foil packet. He tears it open and quickly slides it on.

When he crawls into bed with me, I kiss him instantly.

I've never felt more beautiful or more confident than I do in these moments with Miles.

His lips move to my cheek, to my jaw, then to my chest, where his mouth captures one nipple and sucks. He slides a finger inside me at the same time.

"Oh. I like that," I whisper in his ear.

"If that pleases you, then you're really going to like this."

He rolls until he's on top of me, his hips spreading me wide as he places himself at my entrance, rubbing his head against me.

"Fuck, I love how wet you are for me."

"I love how wet you make me," I say, and he chuckles.

"You just have to have the last word, don't you?"

"Do you expect anything less?"

"No," he says and pushes his head in.

"Shit, I don't think—"

"Breathe, Quinn. You were made for me; I know you were. Just look me in the eyes and take a deep breath."

He pushes fully inside me.

I hiss, but the pain of fitting for him fades quickly.

"Yes, baby, I knew you could take it."

"Oh, wow. You're... this feels so good."

Slowly, he starts to pull out, only to push back in. He goes slow and steady until I'm completely adjusted. When I lift my hips to meet him, his speed increases.

"You're so tight. It's amazing."

I'm too deep in a trance to reply. He brings his knees up to my butt as he pushes my legs open wider so that he can watch himself disappear inside me.

I've never been with a person who not only made sure I was satisfied but who had enough control to slow down to watch what we were doing. To really take the act itself in and enjoy it.

"Sit up," he says. "Look."

I see how big he is, and my orgasm erupts instantly.

"Oh yesssss," I cry out.

With a hand on my shoulder, Miles holds me in place as he slams into me over and over, elongating the length of my orgasm.

"Oh, good god," he groans as he comes right behind me.

He pulses into me twice as he rides it out and then he holds me. He kisses my shoulder and my cheek and my lips.

"I think I went blind for a moment."

"Good," I say, and he chuckles.

He stands and disposes of the condom, walking right back into bed naked.

"I'm not sleeping on the couch tonight," he says as a matter of fact.

"I was hoping you would say that."

And then he rolls to his side, wrapping an arm around me and pulling me close.

I expect to fall asleep and sleep harder than I have in months, but after about ten minutes, Miles makes it known that he has other plans.

And I'm okay with it, because right now, nothing else matters.

CHAPTER NINETEEN

MILES

I quickly sneak back into the bedroom after letting Shadow out for a not-so-quick bathroom break, and I'd do anything if it meant I didn't have to get out of bed again this morning.

Quinn is sound asleep beside me, her back is to me and her hair is draped across my pillows. Man, I thought I loved the way she looked in one of those pajama sets, but Quinn naked is now my favorite look on her.

I don't even care if that makes me sound like some caveman.

This woman is one of a kind, and somehow, I'm the lucky bastard she chose to share herself with.

I glance at the clock, and even though my brain registers that it's past eight and I should have been in the shop hours ago, I have no desire to move. I want to sit here and enjoy this moment.

The reality is, it won't last forever. Knowing that doesn't make it any easier, but it sure as hell makes me appreciate what I have while I have it.

Quinn stirs next to me, then slowly rolls over. As soon as her eyes connect with mine, she smiles.

"Good morning."

"Good morning," I say, sneaking my hand under the covers to grab her hip and pull her closer to me.

She lets out a small laugh and then buries her face in the sheets.

"Oh, don't be shy now," I tell her. "After last night, there are zero things the two of us should ever be shy over."

"I'm not being shy." She lifts her chin. "I'm trying to wrap my head around the fact this is real life right now."

"Waking up next to me?"

She nods.

"I feel the same, but I'll tell you what, I'm loving every moment of it and can't wait to do it again and again and again."

"Hmm, is that so?"

"Yes." I lean forward to kiss her lips and then slowly press her onto her back so that I can roll on top of her.

She spreads her legs for me without hesitation, and I settle there just as I dip my tongue into her mouth.

Morning sex.

Oh, hell.

This is the best.

Her hand slides between us and down until she wraps her fingers around my cock. I swear I grow another size or two just from her touch.

Slowly, her hand moves down and up, her thumb brushing softly over the head before she repeats the motion.

Over and over she does this, and when it becomes too much, I pull my hips away.

She bites her bottom lip.

"You know how much I love it when you play with me, but I'm not coming before you. Now lay back and spread your legs wide. I'm hungry."

Her eyes flash with surprise before she does as she's told.

"Good girl," I growl before I settle my mouth on her.

Her groan is the exact noise I aimed for. I want her to be more relaxed than ever before when we leave this room today.

"Oh, god," she moans after I add a finger to my feast.

She tastes amazing. So sweet, even after the night we had.

I cannot believe I kept myself from this for so long.

"Yes. Please. More."

I add another finger and then flick my tongue faster.

"I'm close," she whispers, and it only fuels me to work harder. I want her to come now, and again when I'm inside her.

She deserves that and so much more.

She deserves to be cherished and worshipped, and I will make sure that's what happens anytime she's with me.

"Ah!" she cries out, her back bowing off the bed. I wrap a hand over her hips and continue eating until her hips stop moving.

As soon as they do, I grab a condom from the nightstand.

I slip it on in record time, but before I can slide in, she sits up.

"Lay on your back," she dictates.

We both know I like to be the one to call the shots in bed, but the look in her eye says I better do what she wants.

Hell, whatever Quinn wants, Quinn gets, as long as it's with me.

I take a breath as I watch her climb over me. The sight of her on top is new, and my cock loves it. The needy fucker is pointing right at her, more than eager for her to sit on him.

My hands rest on her hips; a wicked grin takes over her pretty pink lips. As she lowers herself slowly, her eyes roll at the pleasure she gives us both.

Watching her enjoy me while I'm inside her will never get old.

She starts to move her hips, and thank God for that. I was seconds away from calling the shots.

Back and forth, she grinds on me and then lifts slightly, dropping back down in one quick move.

"Fuck," I say and blow out a breath. "That's it, Quinn. Do that again."

And she does. Twice. A third time. When she goes to do it a fourth, my eyes fixate on her breasts. I sit up and suck one nipple into my mouth.

"Oh, yes," she moans, her movement never stalling.

I switch to the other breast and then back as she rides me.

"I want you to come with me, Quinn. What do we need to do to make that happen?"

She stops, her eyes locking with mine.

"Flip me around and fuck me from behind."

I should be shocked at her blunt words. At how much more confident and comfortable with me she is this morning.

But I'm not.

Instead, I'm a man on a mission to give her what she wants and proud as hell that she feels this way with me.

I lift and turn her, not wasting a single moment as I slam myself back inside her.

"Yes!" she calls out, her back arching and nearly sending me over the edge. "Just like that."

My hips slam against her harder and harder, and within seconds I feel her walls clamping down around me. The suction sends me over the edge with her, and the room becomes nothing but our cries of pleasure.

I pull out and get off the bed to dispose of the condom. When I get back, Quinn is snuggled in bed and smiling at me.

"Now this is a view that will never get old," I say as I crawl under the sheets to join her.

She laughs and covers her face.

"I'm not sure if I'll ever get over this version of you, Miles."

"What version?"

I slide myself right next to her so that I can hold her.

"The version who is more than happy to see me."

"The fucking hasn't made that clear?"

She laughs even harder.

"Oh, it made it very clear how you feel."

"So then why is it hard to believe?"

"Because, we fought for so long, this is something I never imagined for us."

"I did."

"You did?"

I nod. "Well, maybe not exactly."

"Okay, go on." She leans back.

"The first time I saw you was at the ice cream shop. You ordered pistachio ice cream with cookie dough bites. I was fascinated from that moment. I just never did anything about it, and you know the rest."

Her smile grows. "I remember that day. It was my first time in Lovers, and everyone teased me so much that I never ordered it again."

"What? No. That was my favorite part of you. You were so confident in who you were and didn't care."

"Well, I'd posted it online and people hated it. One of my first posts with a string of hate messages came from ice cream. How crazy is that?"

"People suck," I say.

"They do."

"Why did you keep posting if you knew people could be that mean over something so simple?"

"Because social media was how I kept in touch with friends.

Being young and not staying in one place for long meant I didn't get to have lasting friendships, but the ones I did have I could keep up with online. It just snowballed from there. Then I got paid to post, so I kept doing it."

Do you think you'd ever stop?

The words are on the tip of my tongue, but if someone were to ask if I would ever give up my passion, I already know the answer.

I'm not going to ruin this moment today over something I already know.

I hold her tighter and kiss the top of her head.

"It makes so much more sense now."

"What else do you want to know?" she asks.

"Everything you want me to know."

She beams.

"I hope you're ready for this."

Oh, I've never been more ready.

———

"Miles, are you in here?" Hudson's voice carries through the shop later that afternoon.

I grab my towel and wipe my hands as I come around a car to greet him. It's just after lunch and I've barely made a dent in today's work.

As soon as we made it out of bed, Quinn went into the office for an hour, and then I came to join her, where I locked the door and had a midmorning snack on the top of my desk. Then Quinn followed me to the shop where she sat on a rolling chair, with Shadow curled in her lap as she told me all about her first trip with her parents and how scared she'd been to start this new life. She also told me how she fell in love with traveling by the time that trip was over.

Every story she tells me goes to show how you should never judge someone.

Think of all the years Quinn and I could have had if I hadn't been a total jackass.

In a way, it reminds me of Hudson and his relationship with Sadie before last summer. Turns out, being nice can go a long way. It can even change your life.

"Hey." I smile. "You haven't stopped by in a while."

He nods. "I had some time this afternoon, so I thought I'd swing in and drop some lunch off."

He hands me a to-go bag from the bar and looks around the space. I instantly know something is on his mind.

"What's up?" I ask and cross my arms.

He sighs.

"I just came to check on you."

"Why?"

"Because … you and Quinn seem to be getting closer these days, and I just want to know where your head is at."

I uncross my arms and move toward my toolbox to get back to it.

"After all these weeks, you're just now asking me this?"

"Well, yeah. Before you two were faking it, and now that you're not, I just want to make sure you're okay."

"Who says that we're not still faking it?" I ask.

He points at me.

"You. Everything about you says it's not fake anymore. You forget your family knows you, Miles."

The worry etched in wrinkles on his forehead starts to smooth as he waits for me to say more.

"I'm fine. Happy."

Hudson blows out a breath and leans back to rest against the car behind him.

"So, what does this mean? Sadie mentioned a breakup. Don't

even get me started on my thoughts on that. Is Quinn staying here, or is she still planning to leave when summer is over?"

"She's still planning to leave."

"And you're going to let her?"

"Let her? Come on, Hudson, her life is traveling. I can't ask her to change it because we spend one summer together."

"Yes, you can. Trust me, one summer is enough time to know you want to change your entire life for someone."

"That was you. It's not me."

"You don't know that."

"I do know that, because I went into this thing with her knowing she'd be leaving."

"So you're fine with it?"

"Yes."

I don't have a choice. Being okay with it is the only option I have.

"And if she decided to stay, then what? You'd still call it off because you two only planned to spend the summer together?"

I glare at him. Of course I wouldn't call it off.

"Don't make this more complicated than it needs to be, Hudson."

"I don't have to." Hudson pushes off the car and holds his hands up. "I think you're doing a fine job of making it complicated on your own."

I nod.

"We know how it ends," I repeat, as if that should answer all his questions and give him peace of mind.

He shrugs. "Yeah, well, it's not over yet."

Just then the door to the office opens, and Quinn steps out with a giant smile on her face, Shadow following her as fast as his little legs will let him.

He's become addicted to Quinn after just one day, and I don't blame him.

"You are not going to believe what I just saw."

She moves quickly, holding her phone in front of her. She pauses. "Oh, hey, Hudson. How's it going?"

The worry that had consumed his features smooth into a smile.

"It's going great, Quinn. How are you?"

"I'm good. Look," she says and hands me her phone.

There on her screen is a picture of Cherry and Danny cozied up together by the lake. The caption under the photo reads. *This summer with you is my favorite.*

I can't help but smile.

Quinn and I started this whole thing because we didn't want to hurt those two, and now look at them. Looks like this whole thing worked out for the best for more than just us.

I'm about to hand her phone back to her when a notification drops from the top.

They are willing to increase the contract to $60k a year ...

I hand the phone back and pretend like I didn't see anything.

Sixty grand a year for one contract. Holy shit.

How many contracts does she have? She mentioned working with multiple companies.

Fuck. That's not my business, but there is no way she'd give up money like that for life in Lovers.

"Aren't they cute?" she says, looking at the photo again.

"That's great," I say and lean down to kiss her temple. "You did that."

"We did that."

She smiles up at me, and even though she's done it before and even though I said I know how this ends, it still gets to me.

My heart clutches.

I don't want to think of what life is going to be like without seeing that smile every day.

I clear my throat and glance at Hudson quickly before going back to work.

The worry is back, holding heavy in his eyes, but I ignore it.

Quinn and I know what we are doing.

Everything is going to be fine.

It has to be.

I don't have a choice.

CHAPTER TWENTY

QUINN

The past week with Miles has been … gosh, I don't even know the words to describe it. Stress free, maybe? It's crazy. Nothing really matters the way it used to. I haven't been on my phone like I usually am. I'm just in the moment with him, and it's incredible.

I click send on another invoice, smiling because Miles's business is really booming. He's so busy. I love this for him, and I hope that one person can't take all that away from him.

Which is exactly why I haven't mentioned the breakup we have planned for this weekend. The whole point is for us to cut ties from each other so that Mr. Pepperton doesn't do anything crazy.

But maybe since Cherry seems to be happy with Danny, even for now, Miles and I are worrying over nothing.

At the same time, Miles hasn't come in here to talk about it either, so perhaps this whole thing is still filling his thoughts.

I grab my phone and pull up my emails.

My agent sent me a text a week ago, to which I replied that I'd think about it.

Signing another contract with one of the hotel chains I work with. It's good money, but the contract would be for two years. For some reason, that seems like a bigger commitment than I want to make right now.

I read her latest email, with more details and how they need an answer within the next two weeks.

I sigh and flip my phone face down.

My entire life feels like one big deadline. Be here, be there. Don't settle in because you'll be on another plane in just two days.

That's the life I wanted, right?

To turn my love of traveling into something that pays me.

To keep doing what I love for as long as I can.

"Excuse me." The door to the office opens and a dark-haired boy whose face is young enough to put him in high school walks in.

"Hi." I stand. "Can I help you?"

"Yeah, um, my uncle said you were hiring."

"We are. How old are you?"

"Sixteen."

"Sixteen," I repeat. Is it even legal to work at that age?

"I can work the same hours as any adult," he says quickly to my hesitation. "You can look online."

"Aren't you still in school?"

"Yeah, but … it's summer."

I nod. "True, but don't you want to be out having fun with your friends?"

He shakes his head. "I just moved here with my family, so I don't have any yet."

He looks away with that statement, so I don't pry. It's not my place.

"What's your name?"

"Henry."

"Do you know anything about cars?"

"Yeah. I used to work on them with my dad."

"Okay. Are you planning to work when school starts?"

He nods. "Whenever I can."

I study him for a moment.

The last interviews we did were grown men, which isn't bad, but Miles likes his space. A young kid who won't be here all the time might be nice for him. He'll get the help he wants but still have plenty of time here by himself.

"Okay, wait here."

I pop into the shop to find Miles.

When he hears me walking toward him, he turns and grins. As soon as I reach him, he swoops me into a kiss.

"Is it time for a break?" he asks, and I match his grin.

"Miles Asher is looking for a reason to take a break. Boy, look how far you've come."

He laughs at my tease. "You're worth it."

He goes in for another kiss, but I stop. "That's lovely to hear, but there is actually a young man in the office looking for a job."

Miles quickly goes from playful and flirty to business.

"A kid, huh. How old is he?"

"Old enough to work for you part-time."

Miles sighs. "Old enough to know about cars?"

"He says he does. I think you should talk to him."

He rubs his chin and nods. "All right, send him back here. I'll need to see a few things."

"You got it. I'm going to lock up the office and get ready for Grandma Betty's wedding."

He snaps his fingers. "I need to shower for that."

I laugh. "It would be nice."

He reaches out to grab me, but I escape him and return to the office.

"Henry, come on out here."

I introduce him to Miles then finish what I need to before getting ready to go.

Grandma Betty is having a mid-morning ceremony and reception during the week.

Of course she would.

But it doesn't bother me, because as happy as I am for her, I'm more excited to see Miles in a suit.

That I, of course, will be removing later.

———

I DON'T THINK I've ever seen Grandma Betty so happy.

Mike glides her around the dance floor as they share their first dance. She is wearing a cream lace dress, and Mike is in navy blue.

It's a small gathering, but it's perfect. In fact, it's so intimate that I think if I ever get married, this is the kind of wedding I'd like to have. One with my closest friends and family, which, as I'm learning, are the same people.

Maybe not in the local dance studio the way this one is, but still, it sort of fits the idea.

"Does anyone else feel weird that we are at a mid-morning wedding? I mean, I know it's almost lunch, but I've never heard of morning weddings," Miles asks.

Natalie and Tobias both erupt into laughter.

"What?" Miles looks at me. "Was that not a good question to ask?"

"No, it's fine," Natalie says as she wipes tears from her eyes after laughing so hard. "It's just a long story."

"One we would love to tell you someday, but not today," Tobias adds. The cue for other couples to join the dance floor happens, and he grabs Natalie's hand, leading her away from the table.

"Care to join me?" Miles stands and offers me his hand.

"I'd love to."

We are on the dance floor for possibly a minute before Luca walks through, his head down as he hastily makes his way to the door.

"What's he doing?" I whisper to Miles.

"I'm not sure. He's been weird the last couple of weeks."

"Is it because you've been spending so much time with me?"

"No," Miles says and kisses my forehead. "I think it's something else."

Luca is now standing by the door, on the phone. His hands are waving around very theatrically then he shoves his phone in his pocket and walks out the door.

"I think we should follow him." I say and stop dancing.

"Why?"

"He seems upset."

"He's a grown man, and we can't just walk out of your grandmother's wedding."

I ignore him and pull him toward the doors, but when we get there, Luca is nowhere to be found.

"I wonder where he went."

"And I wonder what it's going to take to keep you on the dance floor."

He nuzzles his face into my neck and kisses me softly.

"Well, that's going to get you a lot more than a trip to the dance floor."

Miles chuckles as we return to the reception.

"Is Luca seeing anyone?" I ask.

"Not that I know of, why?"

"He just seemed frustrated, and I feel like it has to be work or a woman."

"Only those two things, huh?"

I nod.

"It makes the most sense. Look at how much I used to frustrate you."

Miles spins me and pulls me close to him again.

"How about we let him figure it out."

"But we are so good at matching people."

"We did it once and for our own benefit. I don't think that makes us experts."

"Maybe a little."

Miles takes a step back and just grins at me.

"What?"

"I love how your brain thinks. Like anything is possible."

"Well, the only other option is to think of things that aren't possible, so why not?"

The song changes, but it's another slow song, so Miles holds me for a little while longer. I rest my head on his shoulder as we sway to the beat.

For the next two hours we eat, dance, and celebrate my grandmother and Mike.

After she and Mike make their exit, Miles wraps his arms around me from behind and rests his head on my shoulder.

"Come on, baby, let's go home."

Home.

Instantly, my chest swells and tears threaten my eyes.

Of all the people who have said this to me, I never thought Miles Asher would be the one to make me feel something.

He holds my hand and leads me to the exit with two squeezes.

Home.

I like the way that sounds.

CHAPTER TWENTY-ONE

MILES

Today is the day Quinn and I break up.

I scrub a hand over my face as we turn onto Main Street, ready to join in on the Fourth of July festivities.

I want a reason to not do this, but I've spent the last three days trying to find a way that doesn't end with things in a mess.

All I can come up with is, no matter what happens, at the end of the summer, Quinn will leave and I won't.

That's the only part of our story that hasn't changed.

And it's best if we accept this is over now. Letting it drag on will only make it hurt more in the end.

This year the town decided that each business would set up their booth right in front of their business so that you still had that feel of walking down Main Street. Also, if someone sees something they like, they don't need to walk around to find the store—it's right here.

Honestly, I'm not sure why they didn't do this sooner.

"What time does the bake-off start?" Quinn asks as we walk deeper into the festival already in full swing. It's only just after lunch, but that's how this town works for these gatherings.

"In fifteen minutes."

"So, we should head right there?"

"Yeah, do you want a drink first?"

"It's basically lunch, Miles," Quinn says with a small laugh.

"And it's the weekend, soooo…"

"So yeah, get me what you're having."

I pinch her side. She squeals and pushes me away from her playfully. "You get drinks, and I'll go check us in for the bake-off."

"Deal."

I lean down and kiss the top of her head, then walk off.

When I look up, Luca is watching and waiting for me in front of Hudson's booth.

"Look who showed up," Luca says.

"I was busy." I walk right by him to go inside the bar.

I could order outside, but it'll be quicker inside because fewer tourists will be there.

"With Quinn?"

"Obviously," I say without looking at him.

"So, how's that going?"

"Good."

A small smile touches my lips. Really good.

"The usual?" Hudson asks.

"Yeah, but make it two."

"Three," Luca says quickly.

"Okay, well, don't think we are making this a summer thing," Luca snaps after Hudson comes back with beers. "Hudson last summer, you this summer, and me next summer. Nope. No thanks."

"Don't be silly," I tell him, and he scowls at me. "Ruby this summer and you the next."

Hudson lets out a deep laugh while Luca just glares at me.

"I liked it better when I was the funny one."

"Really? It's kind of fun. Maybe we should switch. You can be all broody and dickish, I'll crack jokes and enjoy life."

"I think it's a great idea." Hudson adds. "Plus, that's how this summer thing works. You have to be dickish, as Miles said, for the right girl to come around and challenge you."

I smile now, because it's been a while since Hudson and I teamed up against Luca.

"You two are so funny. Not," Luca says and then walks off.

I keep smiling as I wave goodbye to Hudson and head to the bakery. I have a bake-off to win and a breakup to prepare for.

The last thought makes my smile drop and my stomach flop.

With drinks in hand, I weave through people on the street and find Quinn standing at our table, already prepped with tools. She's got her phone out and looks to be filming something. She makes it look so easy. Sharing what you love. I wonder how that would work for the shop. Do I just post about cars and caption it *I loved working on this*? Because if so, that's what I'd put for every single post. People would be bored.

Quinn puts the phone down, so I walk up to our table.

"Get this," she steps in closer, her perfume surrounding me. "Danny and Cherry are at the table to our right, and Hudson and Sadie are at the table to our left. Natalie and Tobias are here, too, but they are up front. I can't believe Cherry and Danny joined as a couple."

I couldn't care less, but the way her face lights up makes me smile again.

She makes me smile.

Fuck.

"Okay, who's ready to get started?" Brooke announces as she walks out of the bakery to the front of the group. She quickly goes over the rules and how we don't have electric mixers because the cords in the street are a hazard, but we have plenty of space in the oven to bake. We can pick between cookies or cupcakes. There will be a winner for each, and the judges for today are the town's favorite old man trio, Bartly, Marty, and Phil. Then she tells us all to get started and disappears.

Quinn and I work quickly, and as soon as I'm mixing the dough into our cupcakes, I ask, "How hard is it to set up a social media page online?"

"That depends on who's doing it. It's really easy to start one and get a couple of pictures up, but it's the maintenance part that gets tricky. Why?"

"What if I set one up for the shop?"

"You should," she replies with a lot more eagerness than I expected. "I can help you do it. I can even help you get a link on there that lets people see your schedule and potential openings. It would be easy to track those who are interested, and you can email or call them based on how they fill out any forms."

I've stopped mixing to just stare at her.

"You have so much content already, and I think the small-town part will be a selling point to clientele who like to remain discrete. You never have to share a name, and I know you don't like to show your face, so you won't need to. It's completely possible to make a faceless account. I mean, it wouldn't hurt to maybe have a post that we can pin to the—why are you looking at me like that?"

I chuckle. "You just sound like you've thought about this a lot."

"Oh, well, it crossed my mind this week."

"A social media page for the shop?"

"Ways to help you so that people like Cherry's father can't take anything away from you again."

She looks away cleaning up our space so that she can stay busy.

Has she been thinking similar thoughts to mine this week?

"Okay, teams," Brooke calls out. "The ovens are ready, so please keep an organized line when you start to come into the shop."

Cherry's red hair flashes right in front of me as she and Danny make their way to the bakery.

"I still can't believe that those two are competing together." Quinn steps up next to me, keeping her voice quiet. "Do you think it could be serious?"

"Maybe," I say, not giving a shit right now what's going on with Danny or Cherry.

Hudson and Sadie are stationed on our other side. Sadie is sitting on the table, and Hudson in front of her, leaning over her crossed legs. She's laughing as they feed each other a spoonful of cookie dough.

My heart swells watching the two of them so fucking in love, they don't care who sees.

Then I look over at Natalie and Tobias. They are each wearing a baby carrier, baby included, as they go over the recipe. Natalie starts to laugh as she holds it in front of Tobias, and he holds up the two eggs we were given. They both erupt into more laughter as they set the eggs and recipe down, clearly abandoning their work. They step closer to each other and kiss quickly.

"All right, I think we are ready," Quinn says, holding up the muffin trays. "Do you want me to take them, or do you want to do it?"

"Let's do it together." I take one of the trays.

"Okay." She beams and then spins for the door.

"Who do you think is going to win?"

"Us, duh. Come on, Asher, have faith."

I chuckle and follow her into the bakery. We make our way to the back and hand Brooke our trays.

On our way out, we spot Danny, Cherry, and her father. Danny and Mr. Pepperton are shaking hands as if they are meeting for the first time.

Quinn makes a sharp inhale noise and grabs my hand, then she pulls me out the door.

"Oh my god, did you see Cherry's face?"

"No."

"She was smiling so freaking big at Danny." Her hand goes to her heart. "Awe, I think we actually did it. We made two people fall for each other."

Yeah, I think we did. But I don't think we did it to just one couple.

I think we did it to ourselves, too.

Which is insane to think about. How can one kiss make you want more? How can one person change your mind about so many things in the time it takes to snap your fingers?

Easy.

Because when it's the right person, nothing matters as long as you are together, and this whole scheme has lasted as long as it has only because I've been doing it with Quinn. Anyone else and I'd have ended it sooner. Hell, I wouldn't have even started it.

Which means only one thing to me now.

A breakup ... yeah, that's not happening.

"I CAN'T BELIEVE we didn't win," Quinn says as she takes a seat outside Hudson's Bar, where he's set up his little pergola booth. She sips her beer with a little scowl, making a wrinkle form on her forehead.

"Yeah, well, don't tell your grandma this, but she's had a lot more years than us to practice."

Quinn's head falls back with laughter.

"I'd love to see you tell that to her face."

"No, thank you."

"Do you mind if we join you?" Natalie asks as she and Tobias walk out of the bar.

"Not at all," Quinn answers. "Where are the babies?"

"Grandma B took them home for us. She said to take an hour or two for us," Tobias says, resting his arm on the back of Natalie's chair.

"I might only make it through one drink. I'm exhausted."

"Me too." Tobias kisses his wife's head just as Hudson and Sadie join us.

Hudson reaches for one of Quinn's and my cupcakes. Red velvet with cream cheese frosting.

I swat his hand away. "No cupcakes for you," I say quickly.

"What? Why not? We made cookies and not cupcakes, so they are gone already."

"No, they are gone because you two ate so much dough, you could only make four cookies."

Sadie and Quinn both laugh as Hudson pouts.

"I haven't seen you like this in a while," Sadie says to me.

"Like what?"

"Like you're having fun."

I jerk my head back slightly.

I want to argue that she's wrong, but she's not.

Outside of the social media question, I haven't thought about work once today.

"I am," I choose to say instead.

Just then, as if the universe said *that's enough enjoyment for you*, Cherry and Danny step out of the bar with Mr. Pepperton, who is looking right at me.

Quinn basically jerks me out of my chair. "This is our chance," she says quickly. "Just go with whatever I do, okay."

She talks so fast and moves even faster that I don't have a chance to say anything in return.

"I'm sorry!" she yells. Instantly, my heart drops into my stomach, and I swear my blood turns hot as I become aware of the watching eyes. "You deserve so much better!"

And with that, she rushes away from me.

My brother looks as shocked as ever for someone who knows what we had is fake. Tobias is glaring at me.

And Marcus Pepperton is still watching me. Only this time, with less glare. This whole breakup is for him but … fuck that.

Quinn is two stores down the street already.

I don't think twice. I chase after her.

"Quinn, wait," I call out, but she doesn't stop.

"No. I'm not what you need, Miles."

"Quinn."

Nothing.

"Quinn!"

Still nothing.

"Quinn, stop!" I yell even louder, and this time her body jumps as her steps come to a halt.

Since she doesn't turn around, I jog until I'm in front of her.

She's crying.

Damn. Those look real.

She sucks in a breath, and it hits me.

They look real because they are. My smile drops.

"Hey, hey," I say and then crouch down to eye level with her. "Don't do this."

"I can't help it," she says quickly. "I want to play the part."

"I don't think you're playing, Quinn."

She takes a breath and blows it out.

"It doesn't matter."

Then she pushes past me.

"It does matter."

"No, it doesn't. This is what works. This is what *will* work."

"For you, maybe, but it doesn't work for me. Not anymore."

"What?" she asks as if she's out of breath.

"I changed my mind."

"You changed your mind. About what?"

"About us." I reach for her hand. I tug her forward a few steps. "I don't want to break up."

"What about Mr. Pep—"

"Screw him."

"But you said—"

"Forget what I said. Forget what I said about everything, okay?"

"I … I don't understand."

I nod slowly, a grin touching my lips as I look her in the eye.

"You want me to be clear, Quinn?"

"Please."

I reach up, threading my fingers into her hair with one hand and cupping the right side of her face with the other.

"Breaking up isn't an option anymore, and fake dating—well, that's not an option either. From this moment on, this thing between us is real. Very, *very,* real."

Her tongue slips over her lips and she bites her lower one.

"So, what's next?"

"Well, I'd like to kiss you again, and then I think we should grab our cupcakes and head home, if that's okay with you."

She gives one small nod.

"Home sounds good to me."

I barely let her get the last word out of her mouth before I press mine to hers. I add my other hand to her hair and deepen the kiss instantly, letting my tongue slip past her lips to tangle with hers. Her moan vibrates against my tongue as I step closer to bring her body flush against mine. Her hands rest on my hips, and she fists my shirt to hold me there.

I swear the entire world disappears at this moment. In a moment where I finally let myself have what I want most. Where I know the rest of the summer is going to be one I never want to end.

I have only a month left to spend with this woman.

I'm not wasting another moment of it.

"Let's go," I say, locking her hand with mine and tugging her toward home.

"Our cupcak—"

"We don't need them for what I've got planned."

"Oh," she says as she speed walks next to me.

We pass everyone quickly, maybe a wave here or there, but there's definitely no room for talking.

We reach the garage, and even though my house is right behind it, waiting isn't in my plans. I lock the door behind us, grip her hips, and lift her to sit right on the hood of my current project. I can't think of a better way to have her right now.

"Here?" she asks as slight pink touches her tips.

I nod. "Are you okay with that?"

She bites her lip and nods. I groan.

"Good. Now lift your hips so I can have the dessert I've wanted all day."

As soon as her clothes are off, I place a hand on each of her knees and spread her legs.

This view—hell, it'll never get old.

"I love the way you look at me," Quinn whispers, and my gaze flashes up to hers.

"I love the way you shine for me."

A wicked smile touches her lips, which I take as my cue to get to work.

And I do.

From the first lick to filling her with my cock and hearing her moans echo off the walls.

I work her all night and then again the next morning

Like I said, my time with her is limited.

I plan to spend every single moment of it worshipping her, pleasing her, making her smile, and anything else she'll let me do.

CHAPTER TWENTY-TWO

QUINN

As soon as I stepped through Brooke's front door, I knew I was going to have a great night. Which is saying a lot, because the past couple of weeks have been truly mesmerizing. It seems so mundane compared to the life I know, but I wake up with Miles next to me, go to work for a few hours, then Miles and I go to lunch or make lunch at the house followed by dessert together. After, Miles goes back to work while I go see my grandmother, my brother, Natalie, and the twins, or I pop into the coffee shop to visit Brooke and Sadie. When I get home at night, I cook dinner and we just hang out. The moments alone talking and just being together, of course followed by our nights in bed, make me feel like life cannot get better than this.

Well, that was until Sadie told me about girls' night as I was leaving Sunday breakfast a few days ago. I've been invited to many things, but a girls' night is new for me.

I actually have girls to have one with.

Inside Brooke's house, there are pizzas on the table, stacks of books, and a bucket of ice that has orange juice and a bottle of Champagne inside.

Wow. They really go all out.

Sadie pokes her head out of the kitchen.

"She's here," she announces and joins me in the living room.

I have no idea who would be here. She just said girls' night at Brooke's was on Tuesday and to come in when I got here.

I set my purse down just as Natalie and Brooke appear.

"I was starting to think that she wasn't going to come," Natalie says as she sips what I can only assume is a mimosa.

"Umm, are you supposed to be here?" I ask in a teasing voice.

"We've been sneaking her in since the twins were two months old," Brooke says.

"And here I thought you've been living this hectic life."

"On every night but Tuesday." Natalie smirks.

She gives me a hug.

"Okay, okay, we will talk romance books and all the things, but first, I need to be the one to bring this up … OH MY GOD, you're dating Miles," Brooke says and then claps. "I swear to god, I thought that man would never find someone."

"I hate to admit that thought also crossed my mind, but way before I started seeing Hudson. Miles just always seemed so grumpy and set in his ways, but not anymore."

The past two weeks with Miles … all I can do is smile.

I never would have ever put us here.

"Do you want to know my favorite part?" Sadie asks.

"What?" I ask when no one else does.

"It's the way Hudson comes home at night and tells me about how Miles asked him to do this or that or when he tells me about something he *did* with Miles. Miles is making time for everyone in his family, and I know we have you to thank for that."

"Oh, I don't think I'm the reason for any of that."

"I do," Sadie argues. "You came to Lovers and changed his

world. Whether it's from helping make his life less stressful in the shop or making him relax at home, he's different."

If we're comparing this to who he was or even who I was at the beginning of the summer, I think we're both different.

"You guys didn't give him enough credit."

"I think," Natalie cuts in, "that Quinn is going to defend Miles all night long, no matter what we say."

"Yes, I will," I say, and the girls laugh.

The conversation easily falls into romance books and how Mrs. Whittaker, the woman who sold Hudson and Sadie the space to expand the bar and open the bookstore, is secretly dating Bartley. Bartley has lived here his entire life and knows everything about everyone.

"Yes, Bartley told Mrs. W. that the marina has not been doing very well this summer and that if Shay can't get things turned around soon, they might have to sell," Sadie says with a frown. "I hate to gossip, but I really hope that isn't the case. I have so many memories out there."

"Even if it sells, it will have to stay a marina, right?" I ask.

Sadie shrugs. "Maybe. With that area, you really have a lot of options."

"I hope Shay figures it out," Brooke says as she tops off all our glasses with the last bottle of champagne. We've had three between the four of us, so it's been a good night.

Why does the name Shay sound so familiar?

"Is this the same Shay that Luca doesn't get along with?" I ask.

Sadie grins and taps her nose. "She's really sweet. You'd like her."

"You hang out with her?"

Sadie nods. "Don't tell Luca. She's normally here, but she said she was working late at the marina tonight, and now I guess we know why."

Silence falls over us as we sit back and relax.

I can't quite place it, but being here right now feels … right.

Being with Miles feels right.

Knowing that he's going to be there when I call it a night feels right.

Natalie is the first to speak up. "I don't want you to leave, Quinn, and I know Tobias would never admit this out loud, but I don't think he wants you to go, either."

My vision starts to blur as tears form.

"Yeah, this summer has been so amazing. It's going to be harder than usual."

"So you still plan to leave?" Sadie asks.

"Um," I say and take a breath. "I have commitments that I made and contracts to complete."

I frown.

Did I really just say that I'm leaving because I have commitments and contracts? Not because I love traveling. Not because I love being somewhere new.

Is that part of my problem? I don't travel for me anymore. My destinations aren't picked based on what I love or want. It's whatever everyone else wants.

At what point in life did I give that up?

Brooke nods. "Do you think you'd ever stop and settle down?"

I nod and answer without hesitation. "I hope I get there someday."

I sip my drink as Sadie says quietly, "Does Miles know you're still leaving?"

"He does."

I look up just in time to see Sadie shake her head as if she's not happy with my answer.

"But I'll be back," I add quickly and with a bit more pep.

The tone in the room is starting to go downhill. "A lot sooner than you think."

Before any of them can reply, there is a knock at the door. Brooke rushes to answer it and Hudson steps in, Miles and my brother right behind him.

"Oh, is this planned this way?" I ask with a laugh.

"Every Tuesday," Sadie says quietly. "You'll be here for the next two still, so you'll see."

Then she hugs me tighter than ever before and rushes out the front door with Hudson.

I know the conversation took a turn to Sad City, but as we all say good night and hug each other goodbye, one thought consumes my mind.

What if I didn't leave?

―――――

"I COULD HAVE EASILY WALKED HOME on my own," I say as Miles weaves his fingers with mine.

I love that all the guys knew when to come to Brooke's. Even Tobias had Grandma Betty stop by the house to watch the twins so he could get Natalie.

From the direction they turned when they left, I think they took the long walk home.

I snuggle closer into Miles's side.

"I'm sure you could have walked on your own, but it doesn't mean you have to."

"Why do you always say that to me?" I ask, pulling away so that I can look at him."

"Because it's true. I'm fully aware that you don't need anyone to do anything for you, Quinn, but I want to do things for you."

I bite my lips to control the smile that wants to take over.

"You're cute," I say.

He chuckles. "Thank you."

The walk is quick and once we get home, Miles pulls me inside and pushes me against the wall, his lips capturing mine in a kiss that says he's missed me way more than he should.

The image of this being our every Tuesday night plays in my head., and I clutch his shirt as if I need to hold on tight just to keep the thought.

"God, I love kissing you," he says when he steps back. He rests his forehead on mine as his hands grip my hips.

"Just kissing me?" I ask, pressing my body into the kiss and giving him what he loves so much.

"Okay, and other things."

I let out a small laugh and look away.

Nights like this mean more to me than I want to admit.

Why hasn't he asked me to stay?

"Hey," he says, bringing a finger to the bottom of my chin and forcing me to look at him. "What's going on in that head of yours?"

I know this is my moment. The one where I should tell him that the idea of staying has crossed my mind. But I don't have all the details worked out yet.

Do I still travel as much but make this my home base to return to between trips?

Do I cut back on travel?

Would I hate that?

Would Miles want a girlfriend who isn't here full-time?

Would he want a girlfriend, period?

I mean, that's what I'd call myself now, but as of this moment, it's all temporary.

The smartest thing to do is discuss my options with my agent before I just go making rash decisions. See if she can find out how I could cut back the travel. If there are any consequences for breaking a contract early. If amendments are allowed in any form.

So I don't want to start a discussion I don't have the answers to, not yet. If I can't make it work, I don't want to get his hopes up.

"Nothing. Maybe all those mimosas are finally catching up to me."

He leans forward to kiss my forehead.

"Let's get you to bed then," he says, and he squeezes my hand twice.

He leads me toward the stairs, but my curiosity gets the best of me.

"You just squeezed my hand twice. You've done that before. What does it mean?"

He pauses and tilts his head.

"Do I keep doing that?"

I nod.

A sweet smile touches his lips. "My mom used to do it to me when my mind was … overthinking. Two squeezes. Two words: don't worry." He lets out a small laugh. "I'd almost forgotten about it until I started doing it with you."

My heart squeezes in my chest.

Oh dear. Don't cry. Not now.

"That's really sweet."

The look in his eyes makes me take a deep breath.

I can't be sure, but I get the feeling that we both have things on our minds that we aren't ready to talk about.

So I reach for his hand and squeeze twice. Then I let him lead me up to the bedroom. "I'm going to take a quick shower," he says.

As soon as Miles shuts the door to the bathroom, my phone pings.

I notice right away that the email is from the travel agency that helps my clients book my trips. I missed the first email from a hotel chain in Germany that I have a contract with for the next two years, so I have to catch up quickly. They want me to visit at either the end of August or start of September in preparation for Oktoberfest, which begins on September 20th this year.

Normally, when I see these emails, I get excited about where I'm headed next. I've been to Oktoberfest before, and it's an experience I'll never forget, but for the first time in forever, the idea of leaving brings me to tears.

CHAPTER TWENTY-THREE

MILES

Do you want to stay in Lovers?

Can you stay in Lovers?

What do you think about staying in Lovers?

Stay with me, please.

Don't leave me.

I groan, stepping back from my current project.

I grab my towel and wipe my hands down, even though they aren't that dirty.

I want to ask Quinn to stay, but I don't know how to do it.

It's the only thing that makes sense to me now, but she hasn't exactly hinted that's what she wants.

In fact, ever since girls' night a few nights ago, she's been … different. Almost as if she's pulling back.

I know her time here is almost up. The day she leaves is like a ticking bomb, reminding us that this thing we have isn't going to last forever.

I hate it.

I hate every moment of it.

A wrench drops behind me, startling me.

Henry picks it up and smiles at me before getting back to work.

Henry is working out great. He's a quick learner and hangs on every word I say. I find this a plus. Ruby was a school nurse before she came back to Lovers, and she said it's so hard to get kids to focus these days.

Knowing this one wants to be here helps. I won't lie. I was a little worried when Quinn told me his age, but then she pointed out that he'd only be here on afternoons and weekends. She knew I didn't want someone in my face at all times, so this kid is perfect.

What am I going to do when she's gone?

Yes, I can do the business side of things fine. Quinn basically made the office work dummy proof, but walking in there to not find her will ruin my day every single time.

Henry will probably quit because I'm a grumpy asshole, then I'll bury myself back into work and put myself right back where I was before Quinn walked into my shop this summer to change my entire world.

Fucking great.

That's what I have to look forward to.

I glance at my watch. It's almost lunch.

I need to talk to someone, and Hudson will be my best bet right now. Luca's been MIA the last couple of weeks. I'm not kidding when I say the two of us pulled a switcheroo.

Guess who's buried themselves into their job now? Luca.

"Henry," I call out. "Want a burger from Hudson's?"

"Ugh. Sure. I don't have cash. Can you just take it from my next check?"

I shake my head. "This one's on me."

He smiles wide. "Thanks, Miles."

"Be right back," I say, even though I'm not sure how quick I'll be. Quinn went with the girls to Wind Valley to look at wedding dresses for Sadie. I want to get my thoughts out before she gets back so that tonight can be nothing but us making a plan.

I can't be alone in thinking that we have to give this a go, right?

It can't just end once the summer is over.

It can't.

Hudson's bar is packed by the time I get there for lunch.

It's been a couple of months since I've walked in here to eat lunch alone. Just another reminder that this is what my life will return to once Quinn leaves.

Unless I ask her to stay.

I've had plenty of opportunities to do so. Every moment with her is a chance to ask, but I want the moment to be perfect. I want to be the kind of man she'll say yes to.

Yet if she were to ask me to give up the shop and my dream so that I could travel with her, I'd say no.

It doesn't seem fair to ask her to do something I wouldn't do myself.

I hate that I'd say no, but my life is here. Everything about me is here.

And her life is travel.

We knew this when we started fooling around, but it doesn't make it suck any less now that the end is nearing.

The truth still remains that I won't know until I ask her, and I need to do it sooner rather than later.

"Miles, hey," a man next to me greets me.

It's Danny.

I quickly glance to his other side for Cherry, but the spot is empty.

"Hey!" I offer my hand. "How are you?"

"Good," he answers on the shake. "Just enjoying the last week here. The summer went fast."

"It always does."

"Especially when you're having fun," he adds. "Which, I wanted to thank you for introducing me to Cherry. I know you two have a past, so I hope this isn't weird."

I smile but hold back my laugh. "Not at all."

"Good, because she's amazing, and I had no idea I'd start this summer as some lovesick puppy over a woman who didn't want me only to end it with a woman I've fallen so head over heels in love with. It was unexpected, but we're headed to Paris next Friday, and I can't wait to make memories with her there. Hell, I think I'm going to ask her to marry me."

"Seriously?" There is no hiding the shock in my voice.

He nods. "Yeah. Crazy, isn't it?"

"Yeah, but good for you," I say and slap a hand on his shoulder. "I'm happy for you both."

"Thanks, and I'm happy for you and Quinn, too," he says quickly. "It broke my heart when she ended things. I couldn't stand the thought of her being alone, but she was very convincing that was what she wanted in life. But now she's found you, and her views on life have clearly changed so I'm happy for her."

"Yeah, me too."

His words hit me right where it counts. It's like I was meant to come here for a warning of what will happen if I ask Quinn to stay.

Silence settles between us long enough for me to order food and a soda for me and Henry. What's the point in asking Hudson for advice now? Danny told me what I already knew.

Danny clears his throat, and just when I think he's going to say goodbye, he surprises me.

"I swear I'm over it, but tell me how you did it."

"Did what?"

"Convinced her to stay. To change her life and pick you.

Traveling has been the love of her life for so long that I truly did believe she wouldn't let someone else in. But she did with you, and I just want to know how."

I swallow the lump in my throat and stare at my drink.

I didn't do any of those things, and he's absolutely right. Traveling is the love of her life, because if she felt even an ounce of what I feel for her, she wouldn't want to leave.

I can feel his eyes on me, so I turn and give my best fake smile.

"It's sort of like you said, this summer didn't go the way I expected. It went better. When you know, you know, right?"

"I guess we both just needed to find the right one."

"Yep."

"Well, see you around Miles. I have a hunch Cherry and I will be back next summer."

"See you around, Danny," I say and wave as he leaves.

Hudson comes up at that exact moment, that same wrinkle between his eyes that he had weeks ago in my garage.

"You were listening, weren't you?"

"Yeah. What are you going to do?"

I sigh and scrub a hand over my face. "I don't know."

And that's the truth. I know what I want to do, but that doesn't mean it's the right thing to do or what Quinn would want to do, too.

———

I'M on the living room couch when Quinn gets home later that night. Her smile at the sight of me makes my head race and my blood turn hot.

It's like my body has this radar when she's near and it comes to life the moment I see her.

"Hi," she says and then stalks toward me.

She leans down to kiss me, and lets her lips linger long enough to climb into my lap, one leg on each side of mine as she deepens the kiss.

Fuck. My body is so responsive to her.

It always is.

Will I ever find this again?

Hell, I don't want to.

I want it with her.

I lean back to break the kiss.

"I need to talk to you."

"Okay." She smiles hesitantly. "What about?"

"About us."

She climbs off me.

"All right."

"I don't really know how to say this, and I've thought about it all day. I don't think there is a right way to say it, and every version was shot right out the door after I talked to Danny about it."

"You talked to Danny about what?" I can hear the defensiveness in her voice.

"You, but it's not—"

"You talked to Danny about me?"

"Yes, but it's not like I sought him out, Quinn. He was eating lunch, and so was I."

"All right. What did you talk about?"

"He asked me how I was able to convince you to stay."

She leans back. "And what did you say?"

"Nothing, because I haven't."

Her expression remains calm.

"Okay."

Okay? That's it. That's all she has to say about that?

"He mentioned how much you love traveling and how he

thought you'd never find something or someone you'd feel as passionate about."

She's chewing on her bottom lip now, but she isn't responding. Her lack of participation in this conversation gets to me more than it should.

"Was he right?" I ask, my tone much sharper than before.

"About traveling?"

"That you'll never find something you love just as much."

There's a spark in her eyes as she opens her mouth. Here it comes—she's about to give me the same line she gave him, then she's going to leave.

"It's complicated," she says instead. "It's exactly what we didn't want when we started this."

"So un-complicate it."

"How? It's my job, and I have contracts to—"

"To fucking hell with the contracts, Quinn. Tell them you want to cancel them."

"This is my job, Miles."

"Find a new one. One with less travel and one that lets you be here."

It doesn't take her any time to snap back, "Close the shop every two weeks and come with me."

"You know I can't do that. People have planned their schedules around me when I gave them my word on their cars."

"And I signed contracts that mean the exact same thing."

I've only ever cried twice in my life. Once when I broke my leg in seventh grade and again when my mom died.

The longer I sit here with Quinn, the chances of a third time increase.

"There's nothing I can do to keep you here, is there?" It's clear neither of us is going to make a sacrifice for the other.

She reaches for my hands and laces our fingers. I pull her until she stands flush against me.

She slowly shakes her head. "I can't just give up everything I've worked for, and neither can you."

"So that's it, huh?" My voice is laced with defeat. "One summer—hell, half a summer—with you, and this thing with us is over?"

Quinn doesn't answer me, but she doesn't need to. It's a rhetorical question.

She leans into me, and I hold her tight.

"Knowing how this was going to end was supposed to be the easy part," she whispers.

I nod and kiss her forehead, keeping my next thought to myself.

No, Quinn, the easy part was loving you.

CHAPTER TWENTY-FOUR

QUINN

My eyes open before my alarm has a chance to go off. I'm curled on my side, clutching a spare pillow against my chest. Miles is right behind me, his hand draped over my midsection as he holds me close to his heart.

I want to close my eyes and go back to yesterday or the day before, maybe even the week before. Back to when I wasn't suddenly leaving.

The timing, though, after our conversation last night is fitting.

If I stay any longer, I'm not sure what may or may not develop between us. I'm afraid we'd make it so terrible to be around each other that every time I come back to Lovers, we'll avoid the other all over again.

I don't want to go back to that.

I also don't know what's going to happen when I do come back. Will we have to face these feelings all over again? Will we just have fling after fling?

I don't want that either.

I know I'd grow more attached with each visit. So leaving as soon as possible is what's best right now, and the email from my agent in the middle of the night asking me to leave today is a sign that it's time for me to go.

"I know you're awake," Miles whispers behind me and presses a soft kiss to my shoulder.

I roll over to face him.

I have to tell him.

Miles thinks we have a few more days, but Tobias and Natalie will be here in a couple of hours to drive me to the airport in Wind Valley.

"I am."

"What should we do today?" he asks, his hand coming to the side of my face as he leans forward. He tries to kiss me, but I turn my head.

I swear to god, it's like I slapped him.

He leans back, his eyes boring into mine.

He knows what I'm about to say.

"You're leaving today, aren't you?"

I nod, and then my tears are uncontrollable.

He huffs and gets out of bed, jerking his sweats on. Then he walks to the closet for a shirt and puts it on, Shadow runs around his feet ready to be let out.

"Do you want breakfast?"

"That's it?" I ask and wipe the tears off my cheeks. "Do I want breakfast?"

"What do you want me to say, Quinn?"

"I don't know."

"Well, neither do it. Which is why I'm going to go downstairs and just … just … fuck."

He storms out of the room. I hear every heavy step as he retreats down the stairs.

I quickly get out of bed.

I knew he'd be upset, but after last night, I thought maybe

he'd be a little happy to have this whole thing behind us so that we can both move on.

I race down the stairs behind him.

"Miles." I come up behind him. His head is hanging over the counter, his arms out wide as if they are the only thing holding him up.

I wrap my arms around him and kiss the back of his shoulder.

"You can't do that."

"Do what?"

"This," he says and moves away from my touch. "The moment you walk out that door, it's over. You're gone. That's it for us. Touching and … and … whatever else doesn't make sense anymore."

He's right. I'd only done it with instinct. He was hurting, and I wanted to be the one to comfort him even though I am the one who caused the pain.

"I'm going to the shop," he says quickly and walks out the door.

I want to follow behind him and tell him it's going to be okay, but I don't know if that's the truth.

Shadow runs back into the house and pauses at my feet.

It's like he, too, knows I'm leaving.

I pick him up and kiss his head.

"You better take care of him for me," I whisper on my way back up the stairs to Miles's room to get ready.

Then I spend the last of my time here packing my things.

Finally, Tobias sends a text that he's at the door, and I make my way downstairs. Both my brother and Miles are standing in the living room.

Just the sight of him watching me move closer has my heart racing.

"I wasn't sure you'd come back before I left."

Miles shrugs. "Despite everything, I wasn't about to let you leave without saying goodbye."

I blink twice, doing my best to keep myself from crying.

I move for my things, but Tobias beats me to them.

"I'll meet you in the car," he says, grabbing my bags and walking out the door.

Miles is leaning against the kitchen doorframe, arms crossed and eyes fixed on me.

This vision of him with his jeans, black T-shirt, and backward hat will live rent-free in my mind for the rest of my life.

I just wish there was happiness in the way he looks at me right now instead of pain.

I move to stand in front of him.

Neither of us says a word.

He reaches for me and pulls me into a tight hug, his arms wrapping around me and holding on as if they never want to let go.

His grip tightens just a little in the last time. The small tug right before he tilts my head back to kiss me, as if he can't control himself when I'm near him, is something I'll never forget.

He rests his forehead on mine and sucks in a breath.

"I'm going to miss you, Quinny," he says, gaining a small laugh from me.

This is how I know it's real love, because when you love the way Miles and I do, we could never let the other one give up their passion.

We could never put them in a position to make that choice.

Before I turn into a blubbering mess, I pull back and give him my best smile.

"I'm going to miss you, too."

He nods, though I notice the way his throat bobs when he looks away.

I take that as my sign to leave, but when I get to the front door, I can't help but look back.

He shoots me the smile that won me over, the smile that warms my heart instantly.

"Go make some more memories, all right? I'll need some good stories when Christmas comes around."

I don't think twice about it. I rush to him, wrapping my arms around him and holding him as tightly as I can.

He holds my hand for a quick moment, long enough to squeeze it twice.

I turn quickly and walk away, tears flowing freely down my cheeks.

The sooner I get back to my life, the sooner the pain will go away.

Right?

CHAPTER TWENTY-FIVE

MILES

She's gone.

She's really gone.

It's such a simple thought, and yet my mind keeps repeating it over and over as if I still don't quite believe it.

But it's true.

Quinn Banks is gone, and I haven't moved from this spot since she walked out the door more than an hour ago.

I'll see her at Christmas, yeah, but what will that be like? Will she seek me out? Will our connection ignite where we left off? Will we be faced with another goodbye like the one we just had?

Fuck.

My heart practically skips at that thought.

I'm not sure I'd be strong enough to go through that again. Hugging her for the last time for who knows how long. Smelling her. Hearing her choked, sad voice. Seeing her cry.

Hell, watching her walk away from me.

Those are all things I will be just fine if I never experience again.

Shadow walks into the living room, his head hanging low as he approaches me.

I lean forward from where I'm sitting and put him on my lap.

"Letting her go was the right thing to do, yeah?"

Shadow doesn't make a peep.

"I mean, she doesn't like to stay in one place for very long. It makes sense."

Still nothing.

"We will just be one of those right person at the wrong time kind of couples, right?"

Shadow picks up his head.

"Do you think we will get a right time?"

The pup licks my face and then curls into a ball on my lap.

I let out a breath and kiss his little furry head.

I just need to get back to work and move on with life. The sooner I do that, the better.

I stand up, hooking Shadow under my arm because he's not allowed to leave me alone right now, and head to the shop.

Once I get there, it's like I don't know what I'm doing. Henry nods his head in greeting, but then gets back to work.

I do my best to do that, too, but it's like everything is happening in slow motion. Is that an effect of a heart breaking? Because as cliché as it sounds, I'm pretty sure that's what's happening to me right now.

I'm just going through the motions because my brain doesn't want to accept that my summer with Quinn is over.

Oh, fuck.

It's over.

I slowly sit on the red rolling chair Quinn took over every afternoon during the last few weeks. I close my eyes to focus, and the reality of my life hits me hard in a flash.

I don't want to go back to the way life was.

I don't want to get back into a routine without her.

I don't want to wake up and not make her breakfast. Or not see her sitting in the recliner, sipping her coffee in the morning while she reads. Or not see her smile the moment she comes home to find me waiting for her.

I want all of that.

I want her there when I come home.

I want to be there for her when she comes home.

I want to …

My eyes spring open and I stand.

Her flight doesn't leave for a couple of hours.

"Henry, lock up and call it a day," I say as I head for the shop door.

"Lock up everything?"

"Yes, I'll pay you for the day and for however long I'm gone."

"All right. Is everything okay?"

"Everything is great," I tell him then knock on the doorframe before I rush through it.

I can't let her go.

She's the best thing that's ever happened to me and I cannot lose her.

I won't.

I meant it when I said loving her was easy.

I'll fight every single day if I have to make sure that's the way we stay.

Whether it's traveling with her or her here with me.

I don't care how we make it work as long as we do.

"Why the hurry?" my dad yells from the back patio of the apartment as I jog across the grass to my house, Shadow right behind me.

I turn, running backward, and yell, "I have a flight to catch."

I barely catch his smile as I resume my route.

I've got a one-track mind right now.

I pull my phone from my pocket and dial Quinn's number.

If there is a chance I can still catch her, I'm taking it.

It goes straight to voicemail.

Shit.

I can still make it. I'll get there on time.

I try her again, just to be sure there wasn't anything weird, but no, right to voicemail.

I skip the steps two by two, sprint to my room, and grab my suitcase. I toss it on the bed and Shadow tries to jump up next to it.

"Looks like you're getting your first plane ride, bud."

Shit, where can I get a travel carrier right now?

"Never mind, you're staying with Luca."

I shoot my brother a quick text and stuff clothes in my bag, jogging down the steps in record time. As soon as I swing the front door open, I jerk back and freeze.

Quinn is standing at the bottom step with her suitcases next to her.

Her eyes drop to the suitcase next to my feet.

Shadow runs past me, his front legs moving as one as he bounds down the steps to her, his tongue flopping around as he bounces.

She picks him up and then nods to my bag.

"Are you going somewhere?"

Her smile hits me right in the chest.

That's *my* smile.

I take one step down and lean on the railing with my arms crossed.

"Maybe."

She nods.

"Care to tell me where?"

"That depends." I move down another step.

Shadow is licking her face like a crazed dog now, and I get it, buddy, I really do.

"On what?" Quinn asks.

"On if I was going to make it to the airport on time."

"Hmm." She takes a step toward me. "Where are you going in a hurry?"

She's even closer now. "The best thing that has ever happened to me was about to get on a plane, and I was going to try like hell to be in the seat next to her."

Her eyes glaze over, and I take the last step toward her. She moves like a magnet toward me.

"Miles, I—"

I wrap an arm around her lower back and pull her against me. My hands thread through her hair as I lock her lips to mine.

This, right here, this connection, this passion—I can't let it go. Ever.

I kiss her with all that I have. Her fist finds my shirt and clenches to hold on, and I swear the porch spins.

This is what it's supposed to be like forever.

Me and her.

But of course, she has something to say.

She pushes me back, her hand cupping my cheek.

"You came back," I state the obvious.

"I did, and I have no idea how we are going to make this work. I just know that I want to try."

"I don't want this to end either, Quinn. If it means waiting for you while you travel, I'll do it. If it means I see you only twice a year, I'll do it. I'll wait for you. I'll never find this with someone else, and I don't want to. I've never loved anyone as much as I love you, and if it means I close the shop from time to time, then that's what has to happen. I'll—"

"My turn," she cuts me off. "The only adventure I want from

here on out is with you. Every day. Every minute, and mostly here in Lovers. I want it all. If you have to be somewhere, I'm there. If I need to be somewhere, you're there. We stay together. Forever."

I grin. Between the two of our confessions, we're going to make this work.

That doesn't mean I can't still tease a little.

"Forever? That sounds a bit excessive, don't you think?" I wink, thinking of the answer she gave to me once after I gave her a similar speech.

She punches my shoulder, but she laughs.

"I love you, too, Miles Asher."

Shadow barks just then, so I reach out to take him from Quinn's arms. He licks my face and then hers.

Looks like everyone is getting what they want today.

"Are you sure you'll be okay staying in Lovers?"

She nods.

"It means you'll be giving things up," I point out. I need to make sure she's fully on the same page as me.

"I know. By the looks of it, it seems you were going to do the same."

"For you, I would. I'm an idiot for not figuring this out sooner."

"You're not an idiot. I should have figured it out, too. But maybe you can promise me that we can take at least one trip a year."

"Deal, and it's going to be more than one because I'd never do that to you. But I'm also not sure where we can go that you haven't already been."

"That's the thing, Miles. I haven't seen them with you."

I wrap my arms around her, pulling her tight, only to spot my dad, Tobias, Natalie, and their twins on the apartment patio. Natalie is crying, and my dad is thrusting a fist into the air.

"I was so nervous coming back just now," Quinn admits.

"Why?"

"Because this all happened so fast, and asking someone to make this kind of change is huge, and I—"

Again, I silence her with a kiss.

"I don't want you to ever be nervous to come to me. If we want this to work, we can't hold back."

"Deal," she says and then she winks at me as she heads into the house with Shadow.

I grab our bags and follow behind her.

It's just like she said. Wherever she goes, I go.

Forever.

Sounds like a damn good plan to me.

EPILOGUE

QUINN

I snap another photo and then burst into laughter.

"Let me see it," Miles says, coming up behind me. He wraps his arms around my hips and rests his chin on my shoulder. "That's perfect."

We arrived in the Maldives three days ago so that I could finish getting some content for one of my contracts. On my way back to Lovers that day five months ago, I reached out to my agent and told her that I needed to amend my contracts with all brands. It was tricky, but she was able to end some of them outright, while others were kind enough to find a new place for me with their company.

For some, I still travel, just not as often, and for others, I'm now the person behind the scenes creating the travel itinerary for the new social content creators.

It's so perfect that I almost don't believe this is my life some days.

Which is why we got here three days ago. I got some work done, and then my parents flew out to join Miles, Shadow, and me for another three days.

I lower the camera and grin at my parents.

Miles laughs harder as he looks at them and spots Shadow digging, the sand spraying both my Mom and Dad.

Miles shoos him away and smirks. Turns out, wherever we go, Shadow goes too. We are a package deal now, and my followers love every moment of it.

"I can't believe we let you talk us into this," my mother says. She and Dad grin at each other.

"Now dig us out," my dad demands.

"Not so fast," Miles says, and my eyes widen as he moves to stand between where both of my parents are buried in the Caribbean sand, looking like a couple of mermaids. "I have something to ask the two of you."

"It can't wait until later?" my mom asks.

"Nope," Miles says. He reaches for my mom's drink and holds the straw for her to take a sip. "You too?" he asks my dad.

Dad shakes his head, and even though he's scowling, it's a goofy scowl. The one where he's trying to be mad but really isn't.

"You see that girl?" Miles points over his shoulder. "I've been officially dating her for five months now, and it's been the best five months of my life."

My heart swells. I feel the exact same way. We chose to stay in Lovers with the exception of two one-week vacations. It's not normal for me, but that's okay. Life with Miles is my new normal, and I love every second of it.

In fact, my parents have come to Lovers twice now, which has brought joy to the others who live there, too. But this trip is the first one where my parents came to meet us for a couple of days.

"I just don't think five months is going to be enough for me," Miles goes on, and my bottom lips drop. What's he doing?

"But the two of you"—Miles points at my parents—"are a

hard couple to discreetly get into a room without Quinn tagging along." He leans in close to them and loudly whispers, "I think she's a little obsessed with me."

I kick some sand at him.

"But I'm more than a little obsessed with her, too, so it's fair. That's why I'd like to ask her to marry me soon."

I gasp, and so does my mom.

Dad is beaming.

"I just need your blessing, and trapping you in the sand, on a beach where you two met thirty years ago, seemed like the best place to do it."

"She told you that?" my mom asks with tears in her eyes.

"And you remembered." Dad is more than impressed.

Miles turns back to me and grabs my hand to pull me close and press a soft kiss to my lips.

"When it comes to Quinn, I don't forget a thing."

I kiss him again, and my dad hollers, "You don't have my blessing yet!"

"Oh, right." Miles straightens and lets go of me. "What do you think?"

"I think if you can dig us out in under five minutes, the answer is yes."

Miles and I share a look and then drop to the sand and start digging as fast as we can.

Once upon a time, I had five minutes to change his summer, and now we have five minutes to change our life.

I'll let you in on a little secret.

Win or lose, I'm marrying this man someday.

Want more from Miles and Quinn?
Please keep reading for an exclusive bonus scene of them in the future here.

BONUS EPILOGUE

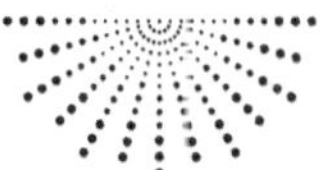

MILES – FOUR YEARS LATER

"I think we need to invest in those cushion seat things," Quinn says as we exit the seating area and head into the main room of Wind Valley's Recreation Center.

My wife waddles in front of me, one hand on her lower back and the other on her round belly.

"Or maybe those seats just suck because everything is uncomfortable right now."

I rub her back and follow behind her.

"If you want a cushion seat, I'll get you a cushion seat."

"Okay, but you have to get one, too," she says, and her tone leaves no room for argument.

Not that I would, anyway. In fact, over the last four years, the two of us rarely fight. Sure, we're still as different as night and day, but that's what makes us so perfect for each other.

"Well, duh, I'm not about to sit in that cold room watching Hudson's team play hockey with a baby in my arms and a hard-ass seat."

Quinn laughs.

"Two babies, don't forget that part."

I roll my eyes and then kiss her forehead.

"How could I forget that part?"

She shrugs. "Your mind these days is just mush. It happens."

I chuckle as I look around to see where the rest of my family went.

Turns out, twins run high in both our families. Now, did we think that it wasn't possible for Quinn to have twins when her brother also had twins? Yes, we did.

Yet here we are, about to have our own set.

Two boys.

Wow.

I can't even put my head around it somedays.

This time next month, our entire lives will be different.

I spot Sadie by the trophy case, holding my niece.

"If she's awake, I want to hold her first," I say, but then Luca is right behind me and so is my dad, who of course pulls the grandpa card.

I'll tell you what, this man loves nothing more than being a grandpa. It's a good thing we're starting out strong with the grandkid count.

"Oh, we should get some popcorn before we go," Quinn says as she walks toward the concessions.

"See you guys back in Lovers," I say to the family and follow my wife.

Like a flash, Dixon comes running past us, and Tobias can barely keep up.

As Quinn orders her food, I can't help but stand back and look at how many people in this room are my family.

I couldn't be happier.

Quinn belly bumps me as she turns. She's already stuffing her face with popcorn, and she smiles.

I kiss her, mouth full and all.

"Think our boys will play hockey?" she asks.

I shrug. "If they don't become addicted to traveling, maybe."

Okay, I'll admit. Traveling over the last four years has been pretty damn amazing, but doing it with Quinn and then coming back to the home we've built together is even better. I have no doubt our kids will fall in love with it, too.

God, I love this woman and the life we have together.

And to think, I almost let her go.

What happens when you secretly agree to help the enemy, and you suddenly find yourself falling for her?
Find out in Luca's book, Tempting Me!

MORE BOOKS BY JAMI ROGERS

For the full list of books and series by Jami Rogers, please visit Jami's website by clicking here.

or

Scan the QR code below.

FOLLOW JAMI

Want more from Jami?

Join Jami's mailing list for exclusive bonus epilogues,
giveaways, and all the book news!

Visit her website
www.authorjamirogers.com

Or join her Facebook group
Jami Rogers Readers

facebook.com/AuthorJamiRogers

instagram.com/authorjamirogers

bookbub.com/authors/authorjamirogers

goodreads.com/jamirogers

tiktok.com/@authorjamirogers

ACKNOWLEDGMENTS

Thank you, Hang Le, Julie, Dana, and Emma, for helping me publish this fantastic book. I'm obsessed.

And, of course, the readers who have fallen in love with this series. THANK YOU!

Cheers to the next book!

ABOUT THE AUTHOR

My name is Jami Rogers, and I write small-town, steamy romance. My favorite tropes to write (and read) are enemies to lovers, friends to lovers, roommates, and my best friend's brother/sister.

I like to read, write, watch movies/TV, and spend time with my family. I'm horrible at returning phone calls and prefer to text, but still struggle to hit the little blue arrow to send a message once I'm finished typing my reply. My husband does 90% of the cooking in our house. Not because I'm busy – I'm just simply a bad cook.

facebook.com/AuthorJamiRogers

instagram.com/authorjamirogers

goodreads.com/jamirogers

bookbub.com/profile/jami-rogers

tiktok.com/@authorjamirogers